ALWAYS

You

A.J. DANIELS

Copyright © 2017 A.J. DANIELS
Cover by Just Write. Creations
All rights reserved.
ISBN-13: 978-0-9958409-3-5

About the Book

ALICE

Eric Knight. He was my best friend from the day he threw sand in my hair when we were three. We were inseparable after that. There were no secrets between us, we never had to pretend with each other--until the day, in our sophomore year of high school, when he told me he was leaving the next morning to go live with his dad on the other side of the country. He promised that once he was eighteen he would come back for me.

Three years.

Three years. I waited for him to come back to me once he turned eighteen. He never did.

Now, fourteen years later he's standing on my doorstep. He doesn't look anything like the boy who left all those years ago--he's taller, bigger, tattooed.

Scarier.

Sexier.

His chocolate-brown eyes still do to me at twenty-nine what they did to fifteen-year-old me.

ERIC

Alice Johnson. I fell in love with her when we were kids. I hated turning my back on her and leaving her in our sophomore year of high school, but my mother was a junkie, and the court decided it would be in my best interest to live with the father I had never met. Turns out my father was the president of an MC.

I've been stuck in that life for the last fourteen years. I wanted out, and I wanted her back. But what I was about to do could get us both killed. Nobody went up against my dad and lived to tell about it.

Enough was enough. I had waited a long time to go get my girl, and I wasn't waiting any longer.

Even in bed my ideas yearn toward you, my Immortal Beloved, here and there joyfully, then again sadly, awaiting from Fate, whether it will listen to us, I can only live, either altogether with you or not at all. Yes, I have determined to wander about for so long far away, until I can fly into your arms and call myself quite at home with you, can send my soul enveloped by yours into the realm of spirits – yes, I regret it must be. You will get over it all the more as you know my faithfulness to you; never another one can own my heart, never – never!

O God, why must one go away from what one loves so, and yet my life in W. as it is now is a miserable life. Your love made me the happiest and unhappiest at the same time. At my actual age I should need some continuity, sameness of life – can that exist under our circumstances? Angel, I just hear that the post goes out every day – and must close therefore, so that you get the L. at once. Be calm – love me – to-day – yesterday.

What longing in tears for you – You – my life – my All – farewell. Oh, go on loving me – never doubt the faithfullest heart.

Of your beloved,
L.
Ever thine,
Ever mine,
Ever ours.

-   Ludwig van Beethoven (1812)

Prologue

I PULLED OPEN my front door, expecting to see Dani and Kat. We were celebrating my birthday with drinks at our favorite Irish pub. But when the door swings open there isn't a five-foot-two, dark haired, emerald eyed female, nor a five-foot-six, brunette with amber eyes staring back at me.

Instead, my honey-brown eyes drift up the six-foot-one frame of a very male body until they connect with his own chocolate-brown eyes. Jet black hair slicked back. His features have a ruggedness to them that wasn't there before. He's taller than I remember. He may not be model perfect, but he always made my knees go weak. But it's those eyes that I would recognize anywhere

Even after all these years, my body remembered and still reacted to Eric Knight, maybe more so to this darker version.

His lips pull up in a small smile. "You don't remember me, do you?"

It's been fourteen years since I'd seen this man, and the sight of him still did to me now what it did to me then.

Only now, he was older and sexier.

"Eric?" My voice is barely above a whisper.

He straightened up, pushing away from the wall he was leaning on, and took a couple steps toward me. Eric leaned down, cupping the back of my head in his hand, and brushes his lips over mine. And just like that I'm transported back to where it all started…

One

I **PULLED AT** the neckline of my dress for what felt like the hundredth time. It's my sixth birthday, and my mother has insisted on putting me in another dress with three-quarter sleeves. I hated dresses, and I hated the stockings I had to wear when I wore a dress.

"Mom," I whined for the tenth time. "Can I please change?" The red and black plaid skinny pants and white Mickey Mouse sweater is the outfit I've been living in for the past little while, much to my mother's disappointment, and it's the outfit I would give anything to change into now.

"No, Alice. It's your birthday. You can wear the dress. Now, please go sit on the couch, and do not get dirty," she called from the kitchen.

"Fine," I huffed, crossing my arms and spinning in my fancy Sunday shoes toward the red sectional in our living room.

It wasn't long until our house was filled with aunts, uncles, cousins, and my school friends, but I'm slightly grateful that the one person I was looking forward to having come isn't here yet. I don't want him to see me in this silly dress. Hopefully, I can still convince my mom to let me change before he gets here.

But then I see his older brother walking through our front door, Eric trailing behind him.

"Happy birthday, Alice," his brother greeted me, and then nudged Eric with his elbow.

"Thank you, Brad."

Brad is ten years older, and was usually tasked with watching Eric and I when I went over to their house for a play date. But him watching us is more like Eric and I playing in the backyard or in the basement while Brad played video games or watched TV in the living room.

"Happy birthday, A." Eric pushed his glasses higher up on his nose and handed me a small gift-wrapped box.

"Thank you, Eric." A blush crept up my face when I remember I'm standing in front of him wearing a dress.

"Brad. Eric." My mother's voice sounded from behind me. "Is your mom here?"

"No, she had to work, Mrs. Johnson," Brad says, avoiding eye contact with my mom, and looking over at Eric. "I'm just supposed to drop Eric off. I'm going to a movie with some friends."

While Brad's talking to my mom, my eyes land on Eric, but his head is downcast and he's avoiding my gaze. Eric told me a couple days ago that their mom had lost her job again, and he was scared because she started drinking more. He didn't want to have to move across the country and live with their dad. But he said Brad told him that would never happen--they wouldn't be going anywhere.

"Well, that's too bad. Alice, why don't you and Eric go join your cousins and your other friends in the basement?"

"Okay, Mom." Spinning on the balls of my feet I led us to the top of the stairs where the sounds of laughter and kids playing floated up from downstairs.

"Open your present," Eric whispered in my ear before we make our descent.

He didn't need to tell me twice. I loved opening presents. I would often ask my parents if I could open their Christmas presents for them because I loved it that much. My small hands ripped at the wrapping paper until it fell away and I was left with a small plain white box.

I look questionably over at Eric but he doesn't give anything away so I hurriedly open the box, and when I tip it upside down a small plastic police badge falls out. My eyes light up at the sight of it. Our favorite game to play together is 'cops and robbers'. Eric and I loved it so much that we decided to make me a pretend police wallet with a paper badge in it, along with the ID card and everything.

"Now you have an actual badge for your wallet, A. Just like the movies." He grinned.

"Just like the movies," I repeated, smiling.

Two

"**B**RAD'S LEAVING IN** five months," Eric says solemnly as we dragged our sleds back up the snowy hill next to his house.

It had been snowing for almost the whole week, which was weird for Oceanview. We're in the valley--it normally hardly ever snows here. Eric and I were making the most of it, and fished our sleds out of my dad's garage first thing this morning. Dad wasn't too happy that we woke him up early on a Saturday though.

"Where's he going?"

"College in Vancouver. I don't remember the name, but I heard him talking to Mom."

"He's going to college?"

Eric nodded. "He got a full scholarship. Whatever that means. He and his friends are going down at the beginning of the summer to find an apartment and get used to the city before school starts in September."

"Huh, that's cool." I moved my sled back into the perfect position to go down the hill and sit down.

"Yeah, I guess." Eric said, wiping the fog from his glasses before sitting down on his own sled.

We raced each other down the hill a few more times before we got bored and decided to make a snowman, which turned into an ultimate snow ball fight. Eric threw his last one and it lands perfectly in the hood of my snow suit jacket. Before I can get it out he ran up to me and pulled my hood up and over my head.

Cold. So cold.

"Eric!" When I got my hood off and the majority of the snow out of my hair I turned to face him, but he's doubled over laughing. His face red from the cold.

"Meanie!" I stuck my tongue out at him but that caused him to laugh harder.

"You should've seen your face," he manages to get out between bursts of laughter.

My brows knit together as I crouched down and gathered some snow in between my gloves. As soon as he sees what I'm doing, his laughter stops almost immediately, and his hands shoot up in front of him while he backed away slowly. Once I'm satisfied with the amount of snow I've gathered I stand and start forming it into a perfect circle.

"Alice…" He was still backing away.

When I looked over at him with an eyebrow raised he turns and dashes for the nearest tree. Laughing, I take off after him until a snowball lands right in the middle of my jacket causing me to drop the one in my hand. Eric is laughing so hard he's giving away his hiding spot.

Our snowball war continued until the sun starts setting behind the houses on our street. The rule in my house is that I can stay out as long as I want, until the sun starts setting or the streetlights turn on.

Eric and I walk back over to the hill to get our sleds before making our way out of the park toward his house.

"I don't want him to go away, A," Eric confides when his front yard comes into view.

"He'll be back for holidays, E," I try to reassure him.

"I know." He sighs, looking dreadfully up his front walkway to his house.

My heart breaks for him because when his older brother leaves, Eric will be on his own. Sure, his mom would still technically be there but she hasn't taken care of him in a long time. It's Brad who makes sure Eric has a bath and clean clothes for school. It's Brad who makes sure Eric has something to eat and his homework is done. Which makes me wonder what made him decide to go to school four hours away in Vancouver.

"I'll see ya at school on Monday, E," I say, starting to make my way down the street to my house.

***

"Give me back my glasses, Gary."

Eric's voice carries out from the lunch room and into the hallway. I hate Gary. He's always picking on Eric, making fun of him for wearing glasses and calling him four eyes. It makes me mad that he and his friends are constantly teasing and bullying Eric for it. What I hate even more than that is when I walk into the lunch room and the rest of our grade is joining Gary in his bullying. No one is standing up for Eric.

But I will.

"Give them back to him, Gary." I march right up to him and put my hands on my hips.

"Oooo, is your girlfriend standing up for you?" Gary sing-songs.

My lips pull up in a smirk. The thought of kicking him where the sun doesn't shine pops into my head for a split second before I shake it off.

"I'm not his girlfriend. And you're a bully." Gary's eyes go wide when I poke my finger hard into his chest. Everyone always underestimates my strength. I may be small for my age, but I'm strong.

"Let's go, Alice. He's not worth it." Eric tugs on my arm, leading me away from the group.

"Yeah! Run and hide behind your little girlfriend, four eyes!" Gary hollers behind us.

"Alice," Eric warns when I stop dead in my tracks. "Don't do it." He shakes his head slightly.

"What? I'm not going to do anything." I shrug my shoulders and slowly walk backward toward Gary and his group of followers.

Eric sighs, lowering his eyes to the floor, but doesn't try to stop me.

"What? Came back for more?" Gary raises an eyebrow, tipping his soda up to his mouth.

"No, I just remembered you had a hard time reaching that really high note in music class this morning and thought I would give you some advice," I say as innocently as I can manage.

"Yeah? What's that?" He wipes his mouth on the inside of his sleeve.

"This," my right foot swings and hits its target. A really high-pitched squeal leaves his mouth as his hands fly down to cover the front of his pants and he doubles over in pain.

"See, there you go. That's what the note should sound like." I spin on my heels, much to the shock of his little group, and make my way back over to Eric. I know I'm going to pay for that later, but I didn't care. Someone had to stand up to Gary and I didn't see anybody else brave enough to do it.

Cowards.

Nobody messes with my best friend. Maybe that wasn't the greatest way to go about dealing with Gary and his group of followers but I'm twelve. I'm not supposed to think before I act yet.

"You didn't need to do that." Eric turns to face me as soon we exit the door to the outside basketball nets. "I could've handled it."

"I know but that's what best friends are for," I lift my shoulders in a shrug.

"The principal will probably call your parents."

"I know." I slip my hands into the warmth of my jacket pockets, suddenly feeling unsure of whether or not I should've taken it that far.

"Thank you." Eric slides his glasses back up his nose with a finger, a slow smile pulling at the corners of his mouth.

***

"She did what?!" My dad's voice carries through to the living room from his office and I cringe.

Guess the principal finally called him.

Now it's a waiting game until I'm called into Dad's office, or he comes marching through that door.

Three.

Two.

"Alice!" His baritone voice booms through the house.

Yup, called it.

"What's going on, Neil?" My mom looks concerned as she walks in behind my dad.

"Alice apparently kicked some poor kid in the balls at lunch today."

Hearing my dad say it out right, without beating around the bush, makes me almost laugh out loud. *Almost.* I'm not that stupid…or brave.

"Alice!" My mom scolds, but she's not trying very hard to hide the amused smirk on her face.

"He was a bully, Dad! He kept teasing Eric about his glasses," I huff, crossing my arms over my body. "And plus, he was having issues reaching a pitch in music class so I was only giving him some pointers."

My mom snorts, and her smirk is now threatening to turn into a full-blown grin.

"Alice," my dad warns.

"Fine, I'm sorry."

"It's not me you should be apologizing to."

Our house phone rings and Mom turns on her heels to answer it. I'm pretty sure the laugh threatening to spill gets let out. Dad eyes her leaving before turning back to me, a huge grin on his face.

"This never leaves this room, and your mother never hears of this. Understand?"

I nod.

"Well done, Alice." Dad laughs.

My cheeks hurt from the huge smile on my face.

"So, did he reach the correct pitch?" Dad chuckles. One of the things I love about my parents is they have no tolerance for bullies, and they've always taught me to stand up for myself and my friends.

"He sure did."

Dad chuckles some more before his face grows serious again. "Alice, I know we taught you to stand up for yourself, and for anyone who's being bullied. And I'm extremely proud of you for doing that. But, kicking someone *there* isn't always the answer. You get that, right?"

I nod. "I know, Dad. But Gary deserved it. It's not just Eric he bullies. And he gets away with it, too! None of the teachers care that he's doing what he's doing. I was tired of it."

"Why do you think the teachers don't care?"

I look tentatively up at my dad, "Because I've told them about what he does, and they haven't done anything about it."

My dad looks like he's lost in thought then he turns back to me, ruffling my hair. "I'll look into it, kiddo. But promise me you won't be going around kicking any more boys."

He's on the school board so I know when he says he'll look into it I can guarantee that he will.

"I promise."

"Good. Now go help your mom with dinner."

Three

2003

AS SOON AS the bell rings to signal the end of the first period classes, I gather all of my papers and textbooks and stuff them into my backpack, not bothering to glance at the English activity sheet we just got back, before being one of the first to push their way through the door and into the hallway.

"Please tell me we're skipping second period," Eric pleads, throwing his arm around my shoulders.

"We're skipping second period." I laugh.

"Yes!" I swear I catch him fist bumping thin air.

"Tough first class?" I tease as we stop at my locker.

"Ugh, you have no idea. Klodnicki is kicking my ass in this class."

"Nice rhyming." I grin, turning to enter the code for my lock. "And you're the one who wanted to sign up for fitness, remember? I told you it wasn't going to be anything like the regular gym classes."

Eric huffs out a breath. "I know, I know. But it was either this or biology. And I could stand to gain a couple extra pounds of muscle." He flexes his arm at the same time he says muscle.

"Okay, Superman. Let's go."

"Hey, you guys skipping second?" Allison asks, skipping up to us.

Damn, is this girl ever not so cheery?

"We're just heading out." I trade in the textbooks in my backpack for the ones I'll need after lunch this afternoon and grab my water bottle.

"Tennis courts?" Logan and Stacey inquire as they join us at my locker.

"Let's do it." Eric puts his arm around me again as we head down the stairs and into the crisp autumn air.

***

"Sonofabitch!" I screech when I get a good look at the english assignment we got back this morning. Once we settled at the tennis courts out of sight from the school, I finally decided that maybe I should check and see how I did on the assignment.

"What is it, A?" Stace asks, trying to peek over the top of the paper where a big red C is staring up at me.

"He gave me a C!"

"Isn't that the one we had to work on with partners?" Allie looks questionably at me.

I nod. "It is. What did you get? I think we did this one together."

She shrugs and then digs around her backpack until she pulls out an identical looking paper. Well, almost identical, because on hers is a big red A.

"If that was a partner project, why do you guys have different grades?" Eric looks over my shoulder passing me the water bottle. The clear liquid burned on the way down when I take a quick sip.

Okay, so maybe there wasn't actually water in the water bottle. Don't judge. Call it peer pressure or whatever.

"That's fucked up," Logan adds, taking the bottle from my hands and taking a couple shots of the vodka.

"Are you going to ask him about it next class?" Stace asks.

"I don't know." I sigh. "Maybe I'll just show it to my dad and see what he says."

We go back to passing the bottle around, and someone lights a joint to go around, too. When the next bell rings signaling the beginning of lunch we all groan, none of us really wanting to give up the spot we've been occupying for the last ninety minutes.

"Want to skip the rest of the day and head down to the lake?" Eric whispers in my ear as we're all gathering our things.

A day at the lake sounds like a glorious idea so I agree. We decide to catch the next bus down to the lake and I pray my mom didn't pick this day to go running by the water.

***

"It's so quiet out here. Peaceful."

"Didn't think it would be in the middle of the day," Eric ponders sitting down next to me.

"I love it."

"Me too." There's something in his voice when he says those words that has me turning to face him.

I'm a little surprised to see him already staring at me. Something briefly flashes in his eyes before it's gone. It happened so fast that I'm not entirely sure I saw it, or what it was. But the way he's looking at me, like he's seeing me for the first time, does something to my body. It's not something I've ever felt before. I like it.

I like him.

Shit, I must have had one too many shots of the vodka if I'm thinking about my best friend like that.

***

ERIC

This is the first time I feel like I'm seeing her. *Really* seeing her. As more than just my best friend.

Alice's light blonde hair shines in the early afternoon sunlight casting a halo around her head. The specs of gold in her eyes seemingly brighter today. The new stud in her nose gleaming in the sun.

She smells good today; like strawberries and cream, and I wonder if she's always smelt this good, and why am I just noticing this now.

I mentally shake myself but I can't help my eyes glancing over at her whenever I think she's not watching. I shouldn't be feeling this way about my best friend. I shouldn't have trouble swallowing whenever she smiles at me. My heart shouldn't race whenever she says my name. And my palms should not become sweaty with just the thought of touching her. Let's not talk about the other part of my body that seems to constantly be at attention whenever I see her.

"You okay?" Her brows draw together in concern.

I swallow hard. "Uh-huh," is all I can manage as she lifts my arm and snuggles into my side.

Best. Friends. I try to remind myself, but then she sighs and presses her soft body further into my side, and it's then that I realize no matter how many times I tell myself we're just friends, I'm still screwed.

I'm thinking of anything and everything I can to try and get the bulge in my pants to go down before she notices.

Four

May 2004

Alice

"**L**EAVE ME ALONE, Scott," I beg, retreating further back against my locker and using the stack of textbooks in my arms as a shield.

"Come on, Alice. One date," he tries again.

Scott is the typical swoon-worthy high school jock. Blond hair, blue eyes, already well on his way to being over six-feet-tall, and he recently made the school's football team.

But I'm not interested.

I'm not interested because he's an asshole and doesn't know how to take no for an answer. This conversation between us has been going on since the second week of school.

Almost two months.

He's been asking me the same question for two months, and for almost two months I've been giving him the same answer. Some might think it's cute, and endearing, and that he must really like me.

I think it's creepy.

"Come on, Alice," he pleads again when I shut my locker.

"Lady said no." Eric walks up behind me throwing an arm casually over my shoulders. "Sorry I'm late," he adds when I look up at him. His chocolate-brown irises reeling me in cause my knees to go weak.

Eric has shot up in height in the last two years; although, he's still not as tall as Scott; however, there's only a couple inches separating them.

It's been weeks since I've seen or talked to Eric. He disappeared off the face of the earth without so much as a phone call or text message. It's not like him to do that and I'm wanting to ask him what was up with the Casper act, but I can't until Scott leaves.

"Tell me you're not dating this guy." Scott hooks a thumb in Eric's direction.

"So, what if I am?" I move slightly more into Eric's side. No one would've noticed the subtle move. Scott sure does though, because anger flashes in his baby blues before he pounds a fist into my locker then stalks away.

"He's still not taking no for an answer, huh?" Eric removes his arm from my shoulders and moves to stand in front of me, casually leaning against one of the other lockers.

"No. The guy really doesn't like competition either." I sighed. "Hey," I playfully push at his arm, "where have you been?"

His eyes go cold. That's not something I've ever seen before. "I don't want to talk about it."

"Eric--"

"I don't want to talk about it, Alice." He interrupts me, his one hand curling into a fist.

I don't know who this guy is standing in front of me, but it's not the Eric I know. I'm determined to get to the bottom of this and figure out why he disappeared for weeks then came back acting like this. For now, I'll humor him. "Okay."

"Thank you." He blows out a slow breath and unclenches his fist. "I'll walk you to your next class."

"I was actually just going to skip it," I lie.

He raises an eyebrow. "Two months into sophomore year and already skipping classes?"

"Yeah, well. After that encounter with Scott I don't think I could sit through a history class right now." I shrug. "He's kinda in that class, too."

"Alright, an early day off it is. What did you have in mind?"

16

I open my locker again and place the textbooks from my arms onto the top shelf, relieved to finally be able to put them down. "I was thinking a walk in the forest across the street."

Eric glances down at my flip flops and quirks an eyebrow.

"I have a change of shoes." I chuckle, pulling out my gym shoes and switching them with my flip flops. "Don't you have classes this afternoon, too?"

"It's just shop class." He brushes it off like it doesn't matter if he goes or skips it.

He's eerily quiet as we make our way back down the hallway of the school and out one of the side doors. We only stop long enough to jay-walk across the street. He's still quiet when we walk past the park to the tree line of the forest.

It's almost a full thirty minutes later when we cross over a small stream and find a fallen tree to sit on, that he turns to me. He pulls a clear water bottle from his sweater pocket, mischief dancing behind his eyes when he uncaps it and takes a sip before handing it to me. I don't think I'll ever get used to the way vodka burns on the way down.

When I look back over at him, his nose is flaring, and he keeps curling his hands into fists, yet his shoulders are hunched forward like he has no fight left in him, even though he desperately wants to fight harder.

"Eric…"

"I'm leaving, Alice."

"What? Why? W-Where?" There are so many questions going through my mind that my mouth has trouble keeping up. He can't leave. He's my best friend, the only person in this world, outside of my family, that I trust. I don't want to imagine a day of my life without Eric in it.

"Mom lost the house. I'm going to live with my dad in Ontario," he says, matter-of-factly. I can tell it's hurting him to say those words by the way his eyes stayed glued to his shoes, refusing to look up at me.

That's what he was afraid of happening when we were six - and when it never came to pass, we were ecstatic. For some reason, we never expected it to come true nine years later.

"What about Brad? Can't you go live with him? That's so much closer than Ontario."

When Eric finally lifts his head and looks over at me, there are unshed tears swimming behind his eyes. "They won't let me, because our dad is still alive."

"They?" I'm so confused right now.

He sighs, and I watch as his shoulders deflate even more. "I have to leave because Mom got arrested and lost the house. My mom's a junkie, Alice."

"Eric." I throw my arms around him and hug him close, wishing I didn't have to let go, and that I could make everything right again.

There's something sobering about having the guy you practically grew up with, who you've only seen cry twice in your life, wrap his arms around your back and grip your hoodie in his fingers while he buries his face in your neck and tries to hide the fact that he's breaking.

"When do you have to leave?" Inhaling the scent of Old Spice original that has comforted me every time I've hugged him since he started wearing it at eleven years old, I slowly disentangle myself from him.

"Tomorrow morning." His voice is barely above a whisper.

"That soon?"

He nods, bringing the bottle to his lips again. "They wanted me to leave today, but I told them I had to come see you and tell you what was happening. Alice, I couldn't leave you without saying goodbye."

"Eric, it's no--"

"Let me just get this out, please?"

I heave a sigh and nod for him to continue.

"A, you're my best friend. You have been my best friend since we were three and I dumped sand in your hair." He grins.

"It took my mom forever to get that out." A half smile pulls at my mouth at the memory.

"You've had my back ever since then, and I've had yours. I wish I didn't have to go. I would give anything to stay here and graduate together like we planned. I've never even met my dad; he split when Mom was still pregnant with me. What kind of person leaves a pregnant woman and a nine-year-old child in the middle of the night?" He shakes his head, trying to dislodge the unwanted thoughts. "I need to say goodbye to you in person, Alice, but I can't bring myself to say it."

Slipping my hand into his, I use the other one to wipe away the tear that escaped down my cheek. "Then don't. It's not goodbye--it's more of a 'see you in three years'. As soon as you turn eighteen, you aren't entitled to stay with your dad any longer, so you could come back. Right?"

Eric squeezes my hand and looks down into my eyes, awarding me with a sad smile. "Right."

I knew that whenever I looked back on this moment, I would recognize this as the turning point in our relationship. The point where maybe it could've turned into something more than friendship if he didn't have to leave in the morning.

"Promise me, Eric. Promise me that when you turn eighteen you'll come back for me and we'll go to college together like we've been planning our whole lives. Promise me."

His other hand comes up to caress my face while he leans in and gently presses his lips to mine. "I promise."

This was it. My first kiss. He tastes like mint and vodka, and I can't get enough of him. I couldn't have asked for a better person to share it with than my best friend.

"Come on," he grabs hold of my hand, tugging me up before handing me the water bottle of vodka. "Let's go to the lake one last time."

***

"Eric," I lean back further into his chest as we both stare out at the sun setting over the water.

"Hmm?"

"Do you think things would've been different if you didn't have to leave? With us, I mean."

I feel all the muscles in his body stiffen for a brief moment, before he sighs and wraps his arms more securely around me. "I don't know, A."

"Would you want them to be?" My heart races with the possibilities of his answer.

"Alice, I leave in several hours. Even if I had wanted things to be different, it's too late now. I would never do that to you."

Moving away from him, I rise up on my knees and throw one leg over him when he straightens his out. Eric's lips part with the forming of a word, but before he can get it out, I press my lips to his.

"Alice," he groans, leaning back.

"Please, Eric," I frame his face between my palms and rest my forehead on his, "I want you to be my first." The rational part of my brain tries to tell me that it's too fast. Losing my virginity shouldn't happen on the same night as my first kiss. But I push the thought away. I can't imagine giving this part of myself to anyone but Eric.

"I'm leaving tomorrow, A." Even though his voice sounds defeated, his hands roam up my back and tangle in the hair at the nape of my neck.

"I know." My voice comes out a little above a whisper as I stare into the depths of his eyes and try to communicate everything I don't know how to put into words.

Eric tilts his face up just enough for our lips to meet in another soft kiss that slowly morphs into something that consumes all of me.

That night, at the lake, with the waves slowly rolling in, and the sun setting behind us, I gave everything of myself to Eric Knight.

And the next morning he left, like he said he would. Taking my heart with him.

Five

May 2007

"**ONE MORE MONTH** and then we're outta here!" My best friend skips up to me, lacing her arm through mine as we make our way out of biology.

"Ugh, I can't wait. It can't come soon enough."

"Please tell me you're coming on the grad trip. Or at least doing ditch day with us," Rachel beams over at me.

Rachel and I became friends shortly after Eric left for Ontario. She was the one who dragged me out of the funk I found myself in after he left. We've had each other's backs ever since.

"Girl, you know it. Sun, surf, and sand." I sigh, picturing the perfect summer we have planned. It was also the summer Eric was supposed to come back. I can't wait to see him again. Three years was three years too long to wait.

"Don't forget the cute guys serving us drinks." Rach laughs, tucking a strand of strawberry blonde hair behind her ear.

"What's this about cute guys?" Logan inquires, throwing an arm around her shoulders and pulling her into him.

"Alice and I were just talking about the summer." Her jade-green eyes dance with mischief when she stares up at him.

"Right, the infamous grad trip." He smiles down at her.

These two had been pretty inseparable since they started dating two years ago. I thought the honeymoon period was supposed to end after the first year. The two of them proved me wrong.

My heart pings with memories of how Eric used to walk up to me in these very hallways and throw his arm around my shoulders. We had so many plans. Get through high school together, graduate, throw the biggest graduation party at Allie's parents beach house before hopping a plane to Riviera Maya, Mexico for the annual grad trip. Then spend the rest of our lives together.

"There's my girl." Scott calls, patting his teammates on their shoulders before making his way to us.

I hated myself for giving into his demands for a date after Eric left, but I needed to get out of the funk he left me in, and Rach thought dating someone might be the best way. It was only supposed to be one date, but he kept asking for another and another, and I was too weak to keep fighting him. We've been dating the last two and a half years, and every time I see Scott I tell myself I'm going to break up with him, then I never do.

I'm such a coward.

I was determined to pull the plug on the relationship this summer, before Eric came home. He would probably kick my ass and give me grief for hooking up with Scott anyway. Rach was right though, it did force me to keep going, to keep living my life while he was gone. I knew he would be even less happy if he came back and discovered I had stopped living my life because of him.

Rachel nudges my arm, eyeing me skeptically. "You might want to stop thinking about Eric before Scott reaches us. You know how he gets, A."

I try forcing a smile but it must look as fake as it feels because Rach's eyes fill with pity.

"I'm sorry," I say on a sigh. "I keep meaning to break up with him but every time the subject comes up he dodges it."

"Why do you want to break up with him? I mean, are you even sure that Eric's coming back?"

It stung hearing those words come out of the closest friend I had, besides Eric. Of course, he was coming back. Why wouldn't he? He had to come back. He promised he would. I didn't have a chance to respond to her before Scott was behind me and wrapping his arms around my middle, his nose buried in my neck. It felt like someone stabbed me in the heart every time he does this. Eric used to do it, and when Scott does a part of me expects Eric's scent to waft up around me, but it doesn't. Instead I smell Scott's Axe body spray.

"Mmm, you smell good, baby."

"Thanks." I try my best to paste on a genuine smile while subtly moving out of his arms.

Scott doesn't notice my fake smile when him and Logan start talking about the football season, but Rachel levels me with a disappointed stare.

Sometimes, I feel like I'm letting her down with some of my decisions or the path I've chosen for my life. *That's ridiculous, right?* If she were as good a friend as she seems to be, then she would be supporting me, regardless of if she agrees or not. Rachel thinks I should stay in Oceanview and go to the local college like everyone else in our group of friends is doing.

"Come on, A. Why don't you stay and go to OVU like the rest of us? I'm sure they have an equally great Social Work program." She crossed her arms over her chest and gives me her impression of big puppy dog eyes.

"I'm sure they do too, Rach. But I've always had my eye set on Ryerson."

"Fine," she huffed. "I just don't see why you'd rather go to school on the other side of the country when the school here offers the exact same program."

I know she means well and wanted to keep our group together, but I've had my heart set on going to Ryerson in Toronto since before I can remember. It was the goal my parents and I always worked toward. And while I knew they would agree with Rachel, they still supported my decision, and reasoning for choosing that school over the rest. Plus, we couldn't live in high school forever. Eventually, we'd all have to move on. This was me moving on from here--if only I was brave enough to give Scott the boot.

***

2 MONTHS LATER

The last month of our summer vacation went by way too fast. Our grad trip to Mexico was a blast, and I wouldn't have traded it with this group for anything. My only wish was that Eric was there.

My throat burns when I try to hold back the tears threatening to spill. He never came home after his eighteenth birthday. When I called, his phone went straight to voicemail, and when I emailed, it bounced back. Mom said that maybe he had also taken a trip this summer, and probably wasn't back yet, give him a few more days. There was still no answer when I called him a couple weeks later.

For the next two months I stalked every obituary column in the paper and online, which was stupid, because if something had happened to him, Brad surely would've called me.

During those two months' Scott started showing his true colors, too. He couldn't understand why I had suddenly withdrawn from him. What he failed to realize was I was always withdrawn from him. I never allowed myself to give all of me to him. Don't get me wrong, we fucked, but that's all it was and it was mostly for his pleasure. I never once got off when we had sex.

I never gave the most important parts of myself to him. Not like I did with Eric. Scott didn't get my genuine laugh, he didn't see me at my lowest. All he got was the girl who was always done up, never in sweatpants or without makeup, he got the girl who constantly pasted a smile on her face, even when it hurt. He got the girl who never allowed herself to show any weakness.

Except when it came to breaking up with him.

We had the biggest fight of our relationship at the end of those two months when he refused to allow me to break it off.

"No."

"What do you mean no, Scott. I'm done. I can't pretend this is what I want anymore." Grabbing my purse, I made my way toward his front door when his hand shot out and slammed the door closed again.

"I said no," he hissed behind me. *"You're not allowed to break up with me. Do you hear me? You belong to me. I own you."*

Turning around within the confines of his arms I shoved him hard away from me. "Okay. One, I am not some possession. No one owns me. And two, I can do whatever the damn I please. If I want to break it off with you, I'll break it off with you. You. Do. Not. Own. Me." I made sure to punctate every last word so there's no confusion on his part. *Who the fuck does he think he is? He owns me? Did we take a step back in time or something?*

Scott's hand connected with the side of my face. My cheek felt like it was on fire, and there was a metallic taste on my tongue from where it ran over my bottom lip. Sonofabitch backhanded me.

Oh, hell no.

When I looked up from under the wave of hair that fell in my face, there's a satisfied smirk on his face. I'm not totally sure of what happened next but my vision clouded with red and when it dissipated Scott was almost fully doubled over with both hands covering his nose. There's a dull throb to the knuckles on my right hand but I shake it out for right now and made a mental note to put ice on it when I get home.

"Don't you dare touch me again."

Before that night, it felt like a part of me was missing. I was always the girl who stood up for others when they couldn't, or didn't know how to stand up for themselves, and I guess I lost that somewhere along the way. That night proved to me who exactly I was and how strong I could be.

My dad hit the roof when I walked through the front door of our house with a busted lip and bruise forming on my cheek. He almost shit a brick when I told him what Scott had said to me that night, then proceeded to high-five and hug me when I told him what I had done. He still called the cops on Scott though.

The crackle of the fire and sounds of conversation around me pull me back to the present.

"I can't believe this is our last night together before we all go off to college." Allie's voice holds a tinge of sadness as she rotates her marshmallow over the fire.

That's another thing that changed this summer. After the whole debacle with Scott, Rachel refused to talk to me. I didn't understand, and I didn't want to drive myself crazy trying to. I no longer gave a fuck. Maintaining a friendship with someone shouldn't have to be as hard as it was with Rachel. A true friendship meant you could go days, months, or years without talking to someone and pick up right where you left off. It did not mean giving the other person the silent treatment for breaking up with her asshole boyfriend.

Logan stopped dating Rachel and hanging out with Scott that day, too. He said he didn't like the guy anyway but thought he would try including him because he was dating me. I wasn't sure if that was also the reason Rach stopped talking to me. Maybe she thought I had something to do with Logan ending it. In truth I saw it coming. The entire time I knew Logan, he always had a different girl on his arm. The fact that he was exclusive with Rachel for two years was rare and out of character for him.

So now, it was back down to the original four before Eric left. Me, Logan, Allie, and Stacey. This was the group I would miss most of all.

"Remember that time at camp in freshman year when we tried sneaking away to go skinny dipping in the lake," Stace grins.

"Ugh, don't remind me," Logan groans leaning his head back against the camping chair.

"Mrs. Cassidy found us as we were coming out of the water." I chuckle.

"And Logan was the only one who didn't run," Allie snort/laughs at the memory and look on Logan's face.

"Yeah, thanks for that, by the way. Even Eric, the bastard, left me standing there...naked...in front of our math teacher." He shivers while the three of us clutch our stomachs in laughter. "If I have nightmares, I'm calling you," he points to me. "I don't care if there is a three-hour time difference."

"Did you ever find out who started those rumors about your um..." Allie's gaze travels down to Logan's zipper, and I have to hold back the new onslaught of laughter that's trying to bubble its way out.

"No," his tone is clipped when he answers her. "But when I do they'll pay. The rest of freshman year was hell after that."

That's it, I can't hold it in anymore. A full belly laugh escapes my throat and I'm having trouble breathing, and I'm not the only one. Tears are streaming down Allie and Stacey's faces as they laugh.

Logan gets more defensive the more we laugh. "It's not funny. And for the record, it most definitely is not small. The lake was freezing that night." He makes a point to grab his package over his shorts and adjusts himself before looking over at Allie. "Tell them, Allison."

Another snort leaves her as she tries to reign in the laughter and paste on a straight face. "It's not small," she clarifies, but when she meets each of our eyes across the bonfire she can't keep it in anymore.

"Assholes. All of you," Logan retorts, jumping up from his chair, beer in hand and stomping back up to the beach house.

"Oh, come on, Logan. You know we love you," Stacey hollers after him.

"Fuckers," we hear him mutter under his breath before he disappears up the walkway.

"I'm going to miss you guys." I didn't mean for that to slip out right here, but it was true, nonetheless. I was going to miss our crazy group.

"You'll call us, right?" Allie asks, grabbing another marshmallow from the bag next to her.

I nod. "As much as I can."

"And you'll come back to visit us," Stace adds.

"Every holiday if I can."

I hated that these were three friendships about to change as well after tonight. I hoped we would all be able to meet up during the holidays I was home, but I also knew that sometimes life got in the way. I prayed we'd still be this close, even knowing that it was inevitable for us to drift apart once we left the beach house in the morning.

***

ERIC

It killed me to have to send Alice's calls straight to voicemail, but I couldn't... I wouldn't pull her into this lifestyle.

I had every intention of going back for her this past summer but after being beaten to within an inch of my life at the hands of my own father not long after moving in with him, I decided that the best thing for Alice was if I stayed far away from her.

A hand slaps my back and if I wasn't always on guard in this place it might have sent me head first into the bar.

"You ready, Junior?" Grim, the club's Sergeant at Arms eyes my half empty bottle of beer before meeting my eyes and tilting his head toward the parking lot where our bikes are parked.

I was far from ready but I would never tell him that. Draining the rest of my beer, I drop some bills by the now empty bottle to pay for our tab before following behind him. All the way preparing myself for the stench of death that was sure to stick to me like glue after this.

Alice may hate me for not keeping my promise of going back for her, but she'd be alive and untainted by my current lifestyle.

Six

Present Day

Alice

I PULLED OPEN my front door, expecting to see Dani and Kat We were celebrating my birthday with drinks at our favorite Irish pub. When I pull open my front door, I'm expecting Dani and Kat to be on the other side, ready to celebrate my birthday with a coffee tour of the city. But when the door swings open there isn't a five-foot-two, dark haired, emerald eyed female nor a five-foot-six, brunette with amber eyes staring back at me.

Instead, my honey-brown eyes drift up the six-foot-one frame of a very male body until they connect with his own chocolate-brown eyes. Jet black hair slicked back. His features have a ruggedness to them that wasn't there before, he is taller than I remember. He may not be model perfect, but he always made my knees go weak. But it's those eyes that I would recognize anywhere

Even after all these years, my body remembered and still reacted to Eric Knight, maybe more so to this darker version.

His lips pull up in a small smile. "You don't remember me, do you?"

It's been fourteen years since I've seen this man, and the sight of him still does to me now what it did to me then.

Only now, he was older and sexier.

"Eric?" My voice is barely above a whisper.

He straightened up, pushing away from the wall he was leaning on and takes a couple steps toward me. He leans down, cupping the back of my head in his hand and brushes his lips over mine. My body instantly heats and then melts into him. A moan escapes my throat.

"Hi." He smiles down at me after breaking the kiss.

"Hi." My head is foggy when I gaze up at him. What was he doing here after all these years, and how did he find me? When was he going to kiss me again?

Apparently, nothing had changed in fourteen years. He was still the only one who was able to light me up with one look or one kiss. And I could still get so easily lost in the endless depths of his eyes.

Like I'm doing right now.

"What are you doing here?" I croak, trying to snap myself out of the trance.

"Aren't you going to invite an old friend in?"

I nod and step aside to let him in. Eric scans the street over his shoulder before making his way inside. That struck me as a little odd but I don't think much more of it.

"Nice place." He whistled, following me down the hall and into the kitchen.

"What are you doing here, Eric?"

"I came to surprise you for your birthday."

"It's been fourteen years, Eric." I move to the opposite side of the kitchen to rinse my coffee mug out and place it in the sink.

Eric doesn't say anything for a while, choosing to watch me from the doorway. "I know," he finally says.

"That's eleven years longer than you promised."

"I know." He mirrors my stance, crossing his arms over his chest as well, leaning back against the doorframe.

It's then that I get a good look at him.

Tattoos cover the entirety of both his arms, arms that are a lot bigger since the last time I saw him. His face is leaner too, having lost all of its boyish charm. My brows furrow when I notice he's not wearing glasses anymore. The Eric I knew used to hate having anything anywhere near his eyes so he avoided contacts at all costs. His dark hair is slicked back. His eyes are more intense, too. It's an intensity that comes from seeing far too much in life, none of it good.

"You changed your hair."

My hand flies to my newly dyed dark locks. I had been a blonde my entire life, until a couple days ago. I was almost thirty, and felt like my life was stuck in a wash, rinse, repeat cycle. So, I decided that it was time for a change - the first thing to go was the blonde. Now replaced by dark brown.

The second thing was I decided to start living for me. I hadn't really done anything I wanted to do in a long time. I chose a school on the other side of the country in hopes I would run into Eric, albeit it was an extremely small chance. And while it was one of the top three schools I had picked out, there were other schools that offered better programs closer to home.

I hadn't finished my degree when I decided to follow Dani and Kat back out to my hometown. The plan was never to move back home, but when Dani needed a quick exit I didn't know what else to do. I knew Mike had eventually become an RCMP officer in town so the logical thing in my mind was to move us all to Oceanview. I knew once here, Mike and his team would be able to keep her safe. Continuing a friendship with Mike was also unexpected. I had met him during his stop-over in Toronto on his way back to BC from Europe several years ago. It was supposed to be a one night thing but we continued to talk once he left and have stayed in touch ever since. It was only once I moved back home to BC that we decided we were much better off as friends.

After that, it was one thing after another. Don't get it twisted--I love my girls, and would one-hundred percent do it again if it came down to it, but now they had their happy ever afters, and it was time for me to find mine.

We stood in my kitchen staring at each other, neither of us really knowing what to say to the other until my phone rang from its perch on the entryway table.

"I'm just going to…" I pointed down the hall at the same time I duck my head and hurry past him.

Kat: Be there in 5.

Oh right, our coffee tour of the city.

I had almost forgotten Kat and Dani were on their way over to celebrate my birthday with me. I sighed, not knowing what to do. A part of me wants to stay and catch up with Eric, and ask him questions--like where has he been the last fourteen years. When he left Oceanview all those years ago he made a promise he would come back after his eighteenth birthday, and that we would never be apart again.

It's not that my life suddenly sucked after he left. Well, in a way it did. Yeah, I had friends, quite a big group of friends through my junior and senior years of high school, and then in college, but I never felt like I could tell them things like I could Eric. All my friendships, aside from a select few, felt superficial, there was no real depth to them.

But a year after he left, all communication from him ceased. One day we were emailing, and texting like normal, and then the next day-- nothing. No emails. No texts. It was like my best friend dropped off the face of the earth. I wasn't even able to contact Brad to find out what happened to Eric because I didn't have his new number.

It hurt knowing my best friend, the person I gave all of myself to, didn't care enough to keep in contact. Or to at least let me know he was okay.

"Got a big date?"

I jump a little at his voice. I was so lost in thought I had forgotten I left him standing in my kitchen.

"Um, no, not really. Just going out with my best girlfriends." I turn to him lifting up my phone. "Look, Eric, I don't know what made you suddenly decide to show up after fourteen years, but I was kind of on my way out, so…" I let my voice trail off again, hoping he would get the message and leave.

I can't deal with this right now. My emotions are so all over the place. I want to tell him he can't just show up at my front door all these years later and expect our relationship to be the same as it was when we were kids. I want to scream that he can't possibly know how it felt to feel like your best friend abandoned you, and being made to miss him every single day when you still have to walk the same halls at school and have to

32

fight the memories of eating lunch together in the halls because the cafeteria was too crowded.

Oh, the things the lockers could say of conversations had in front of them. Seeing him out of the blue with no warning after he broke my heart was too much

I can't bring myself to do any of that because as much as it hurts seeing him again, I'm happy he's here. I'm happy he's not dead, but standing in my kitchen. Eric nods, throwing on his leather jacket. Right before he reached the front door, he turns back to me, longing and regret in his eyes. "I wish I could answer your questions, A, but right now I can't. Come find me when you're done with your birthday celebration. I'll be at our spot at the lake."

It's only when the door slowly closes behind him that I get a full view of an ass that perfectly fills out a pair of jeans, and his jacket.

A Knights MC patch takes up the entire back.

Seven

"**C**HEERS!**" THE THREE** of us clink glasses before we're throwing back another Dr. Pepper shot.

These things are like crack. They don't taste like alcohol at all, and you can usually have a few before it starts catching up with you. The best part is it actually tastes like Dr. Pepper soda.

So good!

"So, let me get this straight. Your best friend from childhood randomly shows up on your doorstep after fourteen years. And he didn't say why he was here," Kat motions for the bartender to refill our drinks as she recaps what I told them.

"Yup." My lips pop at the word.

"Talk about awkward," Dani chimes in.

I nod. "It was."

"What are you going to do?" Dani twirls her finger along the rim of her glass while looking over at me questionably.

I slam back another shot, wiping my mouth on the back of my hand. "I don't know."

"Are you going to the lake?" Kat inquires.

"I don't know." I shrug. "I haven't thought that far ahead," I hold up my empty shot glass as the bartender happens to look over our way.

"You ladies plan on eating anything to soak up that alcohol?" He drawls in that slightly southern accent.

"Three orders of pachos, please Ian," Kat beams.

Usually my stomach would go queasy at the thought of that much cheese, green onions, and bacon on lattice-style fries but after the amount of alcohol I've already consumed and plan on consuming tonight, it doesn't sound so bad. Fried food isn't normally my thing, but heck you only turn twenty-eight once, right?

"I say go. If only to find out why he suddenly decided to show up after all these years," Kat adds her two cents.

"I agree," Dani chimes in.

"He's not the same boy that left fourteen years ago."

"And you're not the same girl who watched him leave, A." Dani lifts a finger in my direction, her hand never fully leaving the rim of her glass. "Plus, I would hope he wasn't the same *boy*."

"I wouldn't even know where to start to even try to catch up on all those years." Another shot.

"The beginning would probably be a good start," Kat smirks.

"Thanks tips." I roll my eyes. "Can we change the subject now," I ask while a server places our plates down on the bar in front of us. "How are the guys adjusting to getting closer to leaving the RCMP, and no longer being on the force?"

Dani shrugs, popping a cheese covered fry in her mouth. "They're liking it better since they don't have to answer to any higher ups anymore. It's not any different than before really. The three teams practically did everything together. For the longest time I always thought they *were* on the same team."

"That's what I always thought, too."

Kat nods. "Jay says the only thing that sucks now are the smaller numbers. But they have Mark and Cole, and I think as long as the five of them are still able to work together, they'll be okay with the downsizing. Plus, Jay's former CO agreed to sign on as well and do some consulting for their new security company."

"Parker's excited about this last case they caught though. They haven't really been needed for awhile, so he's been itching to get out there and solve one last case with all three teams before they leave."

"I hear ya. I told Jay to just go shoot something because he's been driving me up the wall."

A small smile forms on my lips. It's refreshing to hear Dani and Kat happy and talking about their men. For a while both of them were going through one tough time after another.

But so far things seemed to be going well for both of them. *Knock on wood.*

"What are they working on?" My curiosity gets the better of me.

"Some drug trafficking case." Dani shrugs, not going in to detail.

"Jay said they weren't allowed to talk about the details of the case since they have some members going undercover. Not that he talks about the details of his other cases, but this one seems particularly more hush hush." Kat pulls apart two fries before popping one in her mouth.

My stomach churns with the smell of the food and all the grease. I wish I could eat because I'm going to need a clear head if I decide to meet Eric. But that's exactly why my stomach is in knots right now. I had come to the realization that I was never going to see him again. That my teenage dream of one day being with him was never going to happen, and then he showed up out of nowhere.

"Alice."

My head swings to look at Kat.

"Wow, this guy must've done a number on you, A. We've been trying to get your attention for a while now," Dani comments.

"You don't seem like yourself tonight," Kat adds, concern flashing in her eyes.

"I'm okay." I reach out and grab a napkin, wiping my mouth. Fuck, I love this new lipstick, it doesn't wear off or smear at all. Placing it over my barely eaten dinner, I turn to the side. "I think I'm going to go see what he wants and get it over with." I stand, readjusting my mini-skirt and removing my leather jacket from the back of the stool. "Thank you for today, ladies."

"Anytime." Kat smiles up at me.

"Just let us know if we need to hide the keys to the gun safe. You know how protective the guys get." Dani grins pulling me in for a hug.

"I know." I giggle. "But it should be okay."

I pay my bill and give the girls one last wave before pushing open the pub door and heading toward 'our spot' at the lake. It was time to get some answers.

Eight

"DIDN'T THINK YOU** were going to show."
I can feel his chocolate eyes tracking me as I make my way closer to where he's sitting in the sand. His knees pulled up to his chest.

"Didn't think I was going to," I respond, lowering myself next to him keeping my head and eyes focused on the water in front of us, refusing to look over at him.

"You look good, A."

"Thanks." I'm still refusing to look away from the lake and the sun setting over it.

"Are you planning on ever looking at me again?" I don't have to look, I can hear the smirk in his voice.

Taking a deep breath and schooling my features I allow my gaze to move over to his. A slow smile pulls at his lips and when it forms a full smile it takes everything in me to not return it.

"Hi." His voice is deeper than what I remember.

"Hi."

My gaze swings back over to the water as the last of the sun disappears. My heart sinks with the realization that fourteen years ago we were sitting in this exact same place, watching the sun set just as we are now. But back then my heart was filled with hope that what we shared that night was not a goodbye forever, and that Eric loved me, too, because he promised he would come back to be with me. I was a stupid, naïve, fifteen-year-old girl back then. Now, I knew better.

"Are you planning on being mad at me forever?"

My shoulders slump. "Fourteen years," I repeat.

Eric sighs. "I know."

"You never called."

"I know."

"You never texted or emailed."

"I know."

"You promised."

"I'm sorry."

"Why?"

When Eric doesn't respond for the longest time I chance another glance in his direction. My breath hitches with the dark look that's taken over his features.

"Why, Eric?" I repeat my previous question.

Now it's his turn to avoid eye contact with me. His entire body goes rigid, like he wishes I hadn't asked him for an explanation. After sitting in silence and staring at him for what felt like hours instead of minutes I was ready to get up and leave when he finally starts talking, but his voice sounds haunted.

"It wasn't pretty, A. I got involved in some serious shit less than a year after I moved there, and I knew if I tried to contact you again they would use it against me and try to drag you into it. I didn't want that lifestyle to touch you. I wanted to protect you from it."

"What lifestyle?"

He shakes his head trying to avoid the question. It's then that I remember the patch I saw at the back of his leather jacket. The jacket that, I notice, is suddenly missing.

"The MC?" I ask, realization dawning.

"How did you--"

"I saw the patch on your jacket as you were leaving my house this morning. Was it the MC?"

He curses under his breath turning to me, "That's not my life anymore, A. I got out. I left it all behind." His hand comes up to cup my face, his thumb skimming my bottom lip. "I'm here now."

"You're too late," I whisper, willing my body to not react to him.

He scowls. "You got married?"

"No."

His scowl changes to a grin, but he doesn't continue with his questioning.

"What if I have a boyfriend?"

"A boyfriend isn't permanent. A boyfriend I can get rid of."

I jerk away from him but his hand slips around my neck bringing my face back to within inches of his.

"You're mine, A," he growls. "You've always been mine." Then his mouth crushes mine in a heated kiss, and every argument I had at the tip of my tongue evaporates.

Eric's lips leave mine only long enough for him to wish me a happy birthday before they're on me again, then moving to kiss that sensitive spot behind my ear. Shivers rake down my body as I feel his lips quirk up in a smirk before they're back to kissing that spot again, and then his tongue is trailing down my neck to my collarbone.

Ahh, fuck.

His fingers wrap in my hair and he tugs so that my head is forced back a little as he nips along my jawline. He grins when my breath hitches.

"I told you, Alice. You've always been mine," he growls, slipping his hands under my leather jacket and sliding it down my arms. His eyes darken when he catches a glimpse of my tattoo. "You got inked."

"I did."

The tattoo takes up the entirety of my arm from my elbow to the very top of my shoulder. By my elbow is a very detailed picture of a pocket watch with the top open. Roses of varying sizes, starting from the smallest are coming out from the middle of the watch. It almost looks like the roses are transforming and becoming whole the further away they get from the watch.

Eric leans down and places soft kisses on each of the roses before repeating the motion to the pocket watch, his fingers delicately tracing the script.

Time heals all wounds.

I got the tattoo shortly after my twenty-fifth birthday when I finally came to the realization that him leaving hurt me worse than I ever thought it would, and I hadn't completely gotten over the fact that I just didn't mean as much to him as he did me.

His lips find mine again while his arms snake around my back and pull me closer into him. I know what he's doing. He's trying to distract me with his drugging kisses so I won't keep asking him questions. But it's not going to work, not this time.

"Stop. You can't fix everything with a couple kisses, Eric." I pull away from him making sure to add a few more inches between us for good measure. Not like that would stop him.

"Maybe not, but it would be fun to try." His grin falls when he notices I'm failing to smile or budge on my questioning.

"You can't erase fourteen years' worth of wondering where you are, and if you're okay with a simple 'I'm here now', and think that everything will go back to the way it was." I hop onto my feet again, grateful that my buzz from earlier has gone. "Because I have a news flash for you, it won't."

"I never expected it to," he says, standing up to match my stance.

"Then what did you expect, Eric? What did you think was going to happen when you suddenly show up at my doorstep out of the blue after fourteen years of not a word?"

"Well, for starters, I was half expecting to have to beat whatever guy answered the door. I'm not afraid of scaring off any boyfriends, Alice. Know that now. You were always made for me and me alone." He playfully smirks, but I know there's nothing playful about his words. I have no doubt that if there was a man in my life, he would've scared him off.

"This isn't funny, Eric." I turn and start making my way back toward the parking lot.

I didn't make it more than five feet away when a hand wraps around my upper arm and spins me around into a hard body.

Oh shit, he really has grown up.

My tongue absentmindedly licks across my bottom lip before I'm pulling my lip between my teeth.

"Alice," he groans, his thumb pulling my lip free. "You're killing me with that lip biting."

His eyes dart from my lips to my eyes when I bite my lip again. I'm not playing with fire right now, I'm playing with an inferno. I can see the heat blazing brighter behind his dark eyes.

"Fuck, seriously. Keep it up, and I'll have you bent over my bike with my handprint on your ass soon."

My breath hitches at his words. The Eric who left fourteen years ago was sweet, and caring, and attentive. The Eric standing in front of me right now is possessive, protective, and extremely hot. My pussy clenches with the scene he described. And because I don't mind getting burned, his eyes dart back down to my mouth as my lips slowly part and I draw my bottom lip back between my teeth, and ever so slowly let them graze over it.

I didn't think it was possible but Eric's eyes darken even more when he takes my hand and leads me back to the empty parking lot and over to his Harley.

As soon as we reach the bike, he pushes me forward and bends me over the seat so my ass is offered up to him. He thumbs up my short skirt, a groan sounding from him when he realizes I'm wearing a thong, if you can even call it that. He palms each cheek in his hands, the cool air sending shivers down my exposed legs when his hands leave my ass.

Smack!

The pain is instant but short lived, then his hand is back soothing the place where his palm hit.

Smack!

Eric's hand soothes over where his palm hits again before his fingers dip under my thong and into my pussy.

"Eric…" I moan, widening my stance.

"That's it, baby, moan for me. Fuck, you're so wet."

His other hand snakes up my back and tangles in my hair tugging my head back, causing my body to arch and giving him easier access to my neck. His teeth nip at my shoulder before his tongue licks over the same spot and up my neck.

His breath is warm against my ear when he demands, "Come for me, A. I want to feel this pussy clenching around my fingers."

Eric adds a third finger and picks up the pace as he finger fucks me over his bike in a public parking lot.

"Oh, fuck." I groan when the orgasm rips through me.

He smooths my skirt back down, and when I'm positive my legs won't give out under me, I straighten up from his bike and turn to face him. Eric palms the sides of my face and devours my mouth.

"Next time you better believe it'll be my cock making you moan and scream like that." He grins.

"Eric," I slip past him so he's no longer blocking me between him and his bike, "there isn't going to be a next time. While that was…" I gulp and take a deep shaky breath, shutting my eyes "…extremely…wow." For a second I lose my train of thought as everything he did to my body comes crashing back. I don't think anyone has made me feel what he did, not even the purple rabbit hidden in my underwear drawer. And that was with his fingers! My body heats with thoughts as to what it would be like to get the full Eric Knight experience.

The sound of his amused chuckle pulls me back to the present, and I clear my throat before trying to organize my thoughts again. "What just happened…it doesn't change anything."

"You're not going to let this go, are you?"

"No." I tip my head slightly to the side. "Not until you tell me the truth about why you never came back."

"I'm here now, Alice."

"And I'll be here when you decide to man up." Spinning on my heels I get in my car, praying he doesn't follow me this time, and peel out of the parking lot.

Nine

Eric

I HAVE HALF a mind to go after her and follow her back to her place so we can hash this out, but the incoming caller ID has me stalling.

"Knight," I answer on the third ring. "Be there in twenty." I hang up and swing a leg over the bike bringing it to life.

It's going to gut me to have to give up this baby soon, but if this plan worked and I was finally able to be free from my dad's MC then I was getting rid of it. I didn't want any reminders that came from his money.

I pull in to the abandoned warehouse parking lot, and cut the engine. Checking to make sure I hadn't been followed I slip through one of the doors and into the darkened building.

"Collins," I nod toward the silhouetted figure standing just outside of the small scope of light the one dangling bulb from the ceiling offers.

"Knight," he greets, walking closer into the light. Two men flank him on either side.

"Jesus, E. Ever heard of a haircut, man?" Mike chuckles as he emerges behind Parker.

I grin running a hand through the soft strands. "What can I say? The ladies love it."

"Good to see you, brother." Cole slaps me on the back.

"Where's Jay?"

"He had other business to take care of," Parker informs me, crossing his huge arms over his chest and scowling at me.

We haven't exactly seen eye-to-eye since I arrived in town a few weeks ago. Cole was the one who introduced me to the team and convinced them to hear me out. He and I go way back to the first week at my new high school in Ontario. We bonded over football and hockey, and became close friends. He eventually, went on to get accepted into the RCMP and then relocated out here. He was also part of the reason why I wanted out of the club. I always looked up to him as an older brother, like I did Brad, but I knew he was disappointed with the way my life had gone, especially since we had always talked about getting out of that tiny ass town.

He made it. I didn't.

"Thought you weren't making contact with Alice until we knew how things were going to go down," Cole questions, then nods toward Parker when I look at him questionably. "Alice told his woman that an old friend was in town. It wasn't hard to put two and two together."

Ah well, at least now I know the newest reason for the scowl on Parker's face. I knew these guys were protective over the women in their lives, and that included Alice. What we had planned could put her in danger, and possibly cost her her life, but I couldn't let another day go by without seeing her.

I run another hand through my hair, "I had to see her."

Parker exhales hard through his nose and uncrosses his arms easing his stance. "Eric, if they see you with her she's as good as dead, man."

"It's too late to do anything about it now. She's already seen him, and if I know Alice she's not going to let him disappear that easy again," Mike chimes in next to Parker.

"That reminds me. You and I have a bone to pick." I growl at him.

Cole smirks and crosses his arms. "Oh, this should be good."

"Dude." Mike lifts his arms in a gesture of surrender. "I didn't know she was your girl. Plus, you weren't exactly in the picture."

"Well, I'm here now, and don't think I'm giving her up without a fight this time."

"The two of you can have your pissing match later. We need to figure out how exactly this thing with the Knights' MC is going to go down," Parker barks and we all turn to him. One would think that Jay, with all his specialized training in the military, would be the alpha on this team, but he's only the second. Parker, somehow, became the alpha, and when he barks out orders people listen.

"Where do they think you are right now?" Cole asks.

"I volunteered to do a run down here. I'm supposed to check in when it's done. They're expecting a call in the next twenty-four hours."

"What's the next step. Park?" Mike inquires.

"This only works if we catch them in the act. Where do they usually do their shipping and receiving?"

"A port down by the docks."

"Why are they doing business out here when the club is based in Ontario?" Mark interjects.

"Dad started a chapter in BC a few years ago. They're still fairly new, and he doesn't fully trust them with the shipments yet so him, the VP, and the Sergeant at Arms come up whenever there's a big shipment coming in, like this one, so they can oversee it."

"And you're sure it's not just drugs they're trafficking?" Parker asks.

I shake my head then meet his eyes. "I've seen what's in those containers with my own two eyes. It's not just drugs and weapons."

I'll never forget the first time I laid eyes on the 'merchandise' as my dad calls them. Women and children, dirty and bruised, huddled in the far corner of the shipping container. It reeked of fear and human waste, and I hated to think about what some of the members of the MC were doing to them until they were sold.

My father didn't care what his members did, as long as the 'merchandise' stayed alive. It was then and there that my resolve to get out was cemented. I never forgot something like that. That shit stayed with me even years, and countless nightmares later. The sick fucks didn't give a shit about a human life, as long as it made the club money. They did whatever the hell they wanted. It made the satisfaction of knowing I would have a hand in bringing them down even sweeter.

"Fuck," Mike breathes.

I nod. "Before I left, I overheard my dad and his VP discussing a shipment that's supposed to arrive next month. Which means the whole club could be coming down when it arrives. They might even send someone down earlier to make sure everything's smooth sailing."

"Volunteer for that. It'll buy us time to set everything up without being detected. Assure them you have it handled and they don't have to send anyone else down until the day before," Parker instructs.

"There's something else. This club is worse than any motorcycle club you can think of. They don't give a shit about another person's life if they aren't part of the club. These guys won't think twice about taking advantage of those women and children before they're sold."

"Are you saying what I think you're saying?"

Parker's not stupid, and I can see in his eyes that he already knows my answer to his question before I answer.

I nod. "Their morals are nonexistent. They'll fuck anything that walks, especially if they fight back. Those women and children are perfect victims because they can't ever report them. They're here illegally, and nobody would believe them, even if they did manage to get someone to listen."

"Jesus…" Cole says next to me.

"Parker. Man, we have to get to that shipping container before those bastards do," Mike exclaims, his hands fisting at his sides.

There's anger underlying the edges of Parker's eyes as he regards each of us. "They won't be getting their hands on those women and children," he announces, then looks at me. "Go do what you need to do to make sure they don't send someone down here early. Check in with me after it's done." He tips his chin in my direction, then stalks past me out the door of the warehouse

Ten

Alice

INCESSANT KNOCKING ON my front door has me throwing down my book in frustration. I was hoping if I ignored whoever was at my door they would take the hint that nobody was home and leave, but apparently, that wasn't going to happen.

I inwardly groan when I look through the peephole and see who's on the other side. For a second, I war with myself about whether to answer, or to keep pretending nobody's home. If I let him in I can surely kiss my lazy day of reading and relaxing in bed goodbye.

The sound of his fist pounding on my door again causes me to jump twenty feet in the air. *Okay, maybe I'm exaggerating the amount a little.*

"Alice, I know you're in there. Your car's in the driveway."

Frustrated I pull open the door and cross my arms. "Did it ever occur to you that maybe I went for a walk around the neighborhood?"

His mouth lifts in a sexy smirk as his eyebrows rise in question. Bastard still knows me too well. If I was going for a walk, I wouldn't go in the neighborhood. I loved getting out in nature, and a long hike was more my style.

My arms drop back to my sides. "What do you want, Eric?"

He tosses a helmet my way with no warning. I'm lucky I caught it right before it fell with a thud to the floor of my entryway. "Get on. We're going for milkshakes."

"I'm not going anywhere with you. I had plans."

Eric straightens to his full height and peers down at me from behind dark eyes. "Get on the bike, Alice. Don't make me pick that sexy ass up and put it on there myself."

My jaw drops. "You wouldn't."

He moves, bending slightly and getting ready to throw me over his shoulder. I squeak and jump out of his reach.

"Okay! Okay!" Grabbing my keys from the table, I turn and lock the door behind me before putting the ridiculous helmet on. "We could just take my car," I protest, placing my hands on my hips.

"Alice. Get on the bike," he growls.

"Jeez, who pissed in your corn flakes this morning?" I swing a leg over the bike and settle in behind him. Ignoring the way his muscles tighten when I slip my arms around his middle, and press my front into his back.

Being back on a bike behind Eric brought back a lot of memories. In high school, when his older brother, Brad, came up to visit in the summer he almost always came up on his bike. Eric would steal the keys at night once Brad had fallen asleep, and silently roll it to the end of the street until the engine had less chance of waking Brad. He'd pick me up a block away and we'd ride for a few hours without a care in the world.

Of course, when Brad found out what we had been doing he flipped his shit on Eric, saying how he could've killed us both since Eric didn't have his license yet. He calmed down a smidge when he found out Eric really did know how to ride, but it still didn't stop Brad from hiding his keys in a new place every night until he left again for university.

So, when Eric showed up on my doorstep on my birthday with a motorcycle, it didn't surprise me. What did surprise me, however, was the MC patch. I couldn't deny I was curious about how that happened, but I had feeling I wasn't going to like the answer, or any answer to the questions I had about what his life had been like these past fourteen years.

Eric parks in front of a local family owned ice-cream parlour downtown and cut the engine. I sigh, already knowing my meal plan for today has gone to shit. This place has amazing milkshakes, especially their Rolo one. It's thick, creamy, and delicious, and even though they blend it really well it still has pieces of the chocolatey caramel candy. Plus, they add in extra caramel sauce. I'm already salivating just from the thought.

"What can I get you?" The girl in front of the register can't be any older than eighteen, and the way she's looking Eric up and down makes me want to stake my claim on him.

Bitch better back off.

"Can I get one Rolo and one chocolate milkshake?" Eric orders, unaware the girl is blatantly flirting with him.

She's not trying to be subtle about it at all either when she twirls a strand of bleach blonde hair around her finger, and bats her eyes up at him.

"Sure, what sizes would you like?"

Ugh, even her voice is grating on my nerves. It has that Malibu Beach Barbie ring to it. *Like totally.*

Her face falls when he turns back to me and slips an arm around my waist tugging me forward into his side. "What size, babe?" he asks, his eyes on my mouth.

"Large," I respond, making sure my voice has a breathiness to it.

I'll never drink all of it. A large is way too much milkshake, but I'm getting a kick out of watching the girl's eyes go wide and bounce between Eric and me.

That's right honey. He is mine, and he is mostly definitely large.

I turn and shoot her a wink before walking back toward the pick-up counter while Eric pays. She keeps her head down for the entire rest of the time we're there waiting for our order, and hurries into the back room as soon as she hands him our milkshakes.

He chuckles when we walk back outside into the early afternoon sunshine. "Jealous, are we?"

"What?" I ask innocently, playing with my straw.

He stops, milkshake in one hand, and palms the side of my face with the other. His lips are just inches away from mine. "There's no need to be jealous, babe. I'm all yours."

The baritone of his voice has my knees going weak, but I shake it off and take a tiny step back. "I was not jealous. And even if I were…" I tip my head slightly to the side toward the store. "There's no way she could keep up with you. She's just a girl. What you need is a woman."

A low growl rumbles through his throat and the hand that was on my face grips my hip pulling me more into him. "Babe, you're all the woman I need." He tugs me in even closer making sure I can feel the growing bulge behind his zipper. "Are you wet for me, Alice? Do you want me to fill that tight pussy with my cock?"

A whimper escapes me when his hand slips around cupping my backside, and he nips at my jaw before dropping his hand and backing away.

Eric: 1 Alice: 0

There's a playful smirk on his face when he slips his hand through mine and leads us over to the boardwalk. As we walk further along, I tip my chin up and allow the sun to warm my face. Aside from the various mountain lookouts that overlook the city, this was my favorite place in the city. I lost track of how many times I would grab a coffee from the local coffee shop downtown and wander down the boardwalk allowing my thoughts to take over while I strolled along looking out over the water.

A sense of peace settled over me as we walked hand in hand past couples sitting on benches, and kids playing on the playground or in the water park.

"Okay, go ahead and ask whatever questions are running through that head of yours."

I shake my head slightly as we stop at the last bench overlooking the water and Eric tugs me down next to him. "I do have a million and one questions going through my head, but I think I'm okay not knowing until you're ready to tell me."

He places his cup on the seat next to him, careful not to spill it, then leans forward resting his elbows on his knees, his eyes trained on the mountains in the distance across the water.

"I had no idea what to expect when the ministry shipped me off to live with my father in Ontario. When I landed, he wasn't even at the airport to pick me up. He had sent two big guys in leather cuts to retrieve me from the airport and bring me to the clubhouse."

I sit frozen in silence listening to every word coming from his mouth. I can tell I'm not going to like what he has to say.

"Dad was the president even back then. When I walked in, it reeked of booze, and there were drugs and girls everywhere. I didn't think anything of it at first because every MC show or movie I'd seen had their clubhouse looking similar. Hell, I was fifteen, I didn't know better either. At first things were okay, I was still too young to participate or to be a prospect, so they left me alone for the most part."

His eyes squeeze shut against the onslaught of memories and he takes a deep breath before continuing. "Until I found one of the members raping one of the women. I didn't know what was going on at first. All I heard was screaming and someone crying. I went to check it out since nobody was supposed to be there yet. I tried to stop him, like an idiot, but he shoved me back against the wall and continued the assault.

My dad saw what had happened and called me into the meeting room. I thought he was going to tell me he'd deal with it…but instead he hit me until I curled up in a ball on the floor and threw up blood. He took a hold of my phone then and read all the messages I sent you. He threatened to kill you if I ever so much as tried to interfere with club business again." He snorts, absently shaking his head at the memories. *Club business.* That's what they called what they did to those women."

"Eric…" I hesitantly place a hand on his back but he shrugs it off, continuing to stare ahead.

"After that, Dad didn't trust me to my own devices, so I was forced to become a prospect. Prospect is probably not even the right term for what I was. The other prospects had it easy compared to what they did to me."

When he turns to me there are unshed tears pooling in the depths of his eyes. "That's why I never contacted you again. I couldn't allow them to get their hands on you, Alice. I couldn't allow them to do to you what I've seen them do to countless other women. Women are possessions to them. Fuck toys. They don't give a shit about anyone other than the club."

Placing both hands on either side of his face I gently pull him in closer so he has no other choice but to look directly at me. "I get it now. I'm so sorry that happened to you. I wish there was something I could've done."

The pad of his thumb skims across my cheek wiping away a stray tear. "I don't. I don't want you anywhere near that life. It killed me to have to let you go without an explanation, but your life meant more to me. Nobody goes up against my dad and the MC, and lives to tell about it."

His lips brush mine in the softest kiss we've shared since he came back. That causes more tears to fall down my face. The fact that this hard man, who experienced all of that shit life threw at him, and who nobody would blame if he walked around with a chip on his shoulder, could still kiss me with the softest touch.

"Hey." Eric wraps his arms around me and pulls me into his chest. "Please don't cry for me. I'm okay, and I'm here."

Nobody goes up against my dad and lives to tell about it.

His words echo through my head. I pull away and look into his dark eyes. "How did you get out? If nobody lives after going after your dad, then how did you get out?"

He gently pushes a stray strand of hair behind my ear as I'm guessing he's contemplates what to tell me. "I'm taking care of it. But I promise you that you have nothing to worry about. I'll give my life to keeping you safe, okay?"

"Okay." I nod. But it wasn't okay. It was far from *okay.* His dad and the rest of the club could still be coming after him, which meant Eric's life could still be in danger.

I don't know what's about to happen but I know one thing is for sure. I'll fight for him and with him. Even if that meant embracing a side of me, a side of my family, I had hoped to keep hidden.

***

Eric tips his beer back emptying the bottle before placing it on the table in front of us and leaning back in his chair, his eyes studying me.

"So, what have you been up to these last fourteen years, A?"

After our talk on the bench along the boardwalk, I was able to coax him, with very little effort, back to my place so I could make us dinner. He was always a sucker for a good grilled steak. Nothing had changed in that department.

"Er, well, not much. Graduated high school. Went to Ryerson for school, where I met my two best girl friends. We moved here a few years ago when some shit went down with Dani's ex."

When I look up, Eric had stopped eating, his fork suspended in mid-air between the plate and his mouth. I was hoping he wouldn't have heard that little tidbit since I had tried to distract from it by listing other things. But from the look on his face it's apparent he most definitely heard what I had said. I'm not even sure why I said it in the first place though.

He clears his throat and places the fork back down on his plate. "You were in Toronto?"

I feel my cheeks heat when I turn slightly away.

"Why?" His voice comes out hoarse.

I shrug. "I thought maybe I would run into you."

"It's a big city."

"I know. Call it wishful thinking or whatever."

My head snaps up with the sound of his chair scraping against the wood floor. Eric walks around the table to my seat, his hands framing my face when he leans down and kisses me. But it's not the sweet kiss from earlier on the bench. No, this one has more heat and urgency behind it. My body follows his when he straightens back up, but I refuse to let his lips leave mine.

"Alice," he growls.

"I need you. I want you." I grip his shirt in my fingers and try pulling him closer to me.

Our dishes shatter to the floor when he swipes his arm across the table. Then his hands are on my hips lifting me up, sitting me on the table. His fingers run up my thighs. Eric pushes the lace of my panties to the side then he pushes two fingers into me, groaning at how wet I already am for him.

Eric pushes my skirt up higher around my waist and then his hands tangle in the lace and rip them. That was probably the hottest fucking thing I've seen yet. His lips are back on mine as I fumble with his zipper, pulling his jeans and underwear down together.

He pauses for a second, his eyes searching mine for any indecision on my part to letting this happen.

"I'm on the pill."

Whatever hesitation he was looking for, he doesn't find. As the words leave my lips his mouth is back on mine, devouring me.

"Lean back on your elbows, baby."

I do as I'm told, and as soon as my elbows touch the cold wood of the table, he's pushing into me in one stroke. My head falls back and I moan. He is undeniably not fifteen anymore. *Holy shit.*

"You feel even better than I remember," he groans, pulling out so that just the head is inside and then slamming back in again.

"I could say the same of you."

He chuckles, curling his hand behind my neck and pulling me up slightly. "I'm not some inexperienced teenager anymore."

His lips crash down on mine. When he pulls back I nip at his bottom lip pulling another groan from him. "Shut up and fuck me."

"Yes ma'am." He grins and drives home again and again, hitting that sweet spot each time, until we both tumble over the edge and are left sweaty, our breathing heavy.

"I'll clean up here. Why don't you go have a bath?" He says leaning up on an elbow.

"Hmm, sounds good." I'm so relaxed right now that I have trouble standing up, and Eric silently laughs as I struggle to get my legs steady under me.

"I'll join you in the bedroom after I've cleaned up our food and the plates." He slaps my ass and shoots me a wink before going in search of my broom and mop.

Eleven

ERIC

"**I** MISS THIS."

My arm tightens around her shoulder as Alice snuggles more into my side on the hood of her car as we watch the sun set over the water.

"It has been a while since we did this."

For the first time in fourteen years I feel my body relax. Being with her has that effect on me. If I'm stressed, being with Alice makes me relax. If I'm angry or frustrated, being with Alice forces me to take a step back and breathe. She is, and always has been, my happy place. The place I go when I want or need to forget about the world and all its bullshit for a moment.

"How long?" she asks after a while, absentmindedly playing with the buttons on my shirt.

"How long what?"

"How long are you here for, Eric? How long do I have to protect my heart for?"

I shift my position on the hood so I can tilt her chin up with my index finger.

"You don't have to protect your heart from me, Alice. I swear on my life, even if it kills me, I will spend the rest of my days making it up to you, and proving to you how much you mean to me."

Something shifts and changes in her eyes, like she wants to believe me, but she's struggling with it.

"I'm not going anywhere," I growl, leaning down and pressing my lips to hers. It takes all the strength I have to hold back when I feel her relax and open up under me.

Thankfully, she pushes on my chest until I lean back enough for her to wiggle her way out from under me and off the hood of her car. Her arms crisscross over her body as she grips the hem of her tank top and peels it up and over her head. The smile she levels me as the top drops from her fingers is the sexiest I've ever seen, and I vow right here and now to make sure nothing ever dims it. And I pray she always looks at me the way she is now, like I mean the world to her.

I don't deserve the way she's looking at me. Hell, I know I don't. I've seen and done things that will haunt me for the rest of my life. I'm mixed up in some fucked up shit, and if it ever touched her it would kill her, and it would kill me to watch the life dim out of her eyes. I am the last person who deserves the love of a woman like her. It was selfish of me to come back before this mess is cleared up, but I needed her in my life. I was drowning in the darkness, but with her, there was a light at the end of the tunnel. She was that light, guiding me out of the darkness. My only hope was I didn't drag her down with me.

"Alice?"

My head snaps to the side at the sound of the male voice. Instinctively, I move off the car and position myself at her side. The guy moving toward us looks vaguely familiar, but I can't place where I know him from and for that reason alone I try not to interfere. I wasn't joking around when I said she was mine, and I won't think twice about fighting any fucker who got in my way. But I also wasn't a caveman. If this guy was just a friend, then there was no point in getting riled up.

That theory went out the window when I felt Alice tense next to me and subtly move closer into my side. That move alone has my protective instincts on high alert, and I position myself slightly in front of her.

"Scott?"

Everything clicks into place when she says his name, and the memory of this fucker hounding her about going on a date with him most of sophomore year comes crashing back. The way she says his name makes me think that the harassment didn't stop there.

When he's close enough, he stops and peers at her over the tops of his shades. Not giving a fuck that I'm standing right there.

"Wow, A." He whistles. "You still have the sexiest body I've ever seen." He smirks.

A growl sounds in the near vicinity, but it's not until Alice places a hand on my arm and Scott's eyes snap to mine that I realize it came from me.

"Who's the guard dog?" He nods toward me.

"It's none of your business who he is." She grabs my hand. "We were just leaving." Alice slips her shirt back on over her bikini top.

"Aw, c'mon, baby. It's been years since that little incident. Can we put it behind us? Take your guard dog home, and we'll go for a drink and catch up?"

Incident. What fucking incident?

"What's he talking about, A?"

"Nothing." She exhales hard, pulling me along with her and jumping into the passenger seat.

I'm not buying it, something went down between them after I left, and if her reaction is anything to go on, she thinks that if I found out it might result in me kicking his ass. I couldn't do it back then because I was a scrawny kid, but all bets were off now. I turn back to see a satisfied smirk on Scott's face.

"Eric, please. Can we just go?" Alice pleads from her seat.

I get in and click my seat belt in place before starting up her car and peeling out of the parking lot. As we get closer to her house, Alice starts fidgeting more.

Looks like we still have a lot to talk about. *So much for a relaxing day.*

"What incident was he talking about, Alice?"

I follow behind her when she enters her house and makes a beeline for her freezer, pulling out a bottle of JD.

"It wasn't a big deal," she says before slamming a shot of amber liquid. "And I handled it." She wipes her mouth on the back of her hand using the other to pour herself another shot.

Crossing my arms over my chest I force myself to visibly relax and settle against the breakfast bar. I may not have seen her in fourteen years, but I still know how to make her squirm. Not a lot of people know that while she pretends to be this badass in public, it doesn't take very much to make her sing like a canary.

"It's not going to work this time, Eric."

"I'm just standing here." My shoulder lifts slightly and then relaxes again.

"Say something," she presses.

"What do you want me to say, A? You said there wasn't an incident and I believe you."

Our little game goes back and forth until we're staring each other down.

"Fine," she huffs. "But you're going to need a drink first."

She pours us both a few fingers worth of whiskey in our glasses, and doesn't wait for me to grab mine before she's slamming hers back and leaning a hip into the counter.

"Scott and I kinda dated after you left."

I'm pretty sure whiskey is not supposed to go up your nose, but holy f, that shit burns like a motherfucker.

"Jesus Christ, you couldn't have warned me before I shot that back?" I sputter.

"Nope," she answers, a playful smirk on her face.

When I can breathe again I straighten to my full height and move off the counter. "I'm guessing that's not the incident?"

"About six months after you left I couldn't handle him constantly asking me on a date, so I gave in. It was only supposed to be one date, but one date turned into two, and then three. And then it was just comfortable. A year into our relationship he started changing, it was subtle at first, but by the second year mark the controlling got worse."

She pauses, slamming back another shot before continuing.

"When I tried leaving he hit me. That was also the day I learned that my right hook was still as good as it always had been. Part of me wanted to hit him where it would really hurt but Scott is, and always was, obsessed with his looks. Now his nose is not so perfect anymore. It gives me a small piece of satisfaction knowing it's because of me."

"He deserved a lot more than a broken nose."

She nods, suddenly way more focused on the empty glass in her hands, like if she stares at it long enough or hard enough it'll magically transport her away from here.

Smoothing my hand over hers I slip the glass from her fingers and place it on the counter behind her. She's still refusing to look up at me so I tip her head back with a finger under a chin and kiss her.

"Do you trust me?" I whisper in her ear.

When she tips her chin in a slight nod I take that as my cue, and go about collecting the items I need from her pantry before gripping her hand in mine and leading her toward the back of the house and her bedroom.

Twelve

Alice

ERIC LEADS ME into my bedroom and leaves me standing in the middle of the room as he goes about putting the items in his arms on the table beside the bed.

"Strip, then lie down on your stomach in the middle of the bed," he commands, his voice low.

I do as he says, but leave my panties on, and then crawl to the middle of the bed. When I'm on my stomach I feel the bed dip. Eric straddle my legs, careful not to put his full weight on me.

A cold liquid dribbles over my shoulders and down my back, but warms up soon after he starts massaging it into and up my back. I've never had a massage before, but if it was like this every time, then I was making a mental note to get one more often. Especially if it was from Eric.

My nipples harden to peaks underneath me, and a shiver races down my spine from the feel of his callused hands massaging and caressing my body. This is probably the most relaxed I've felt in years. Heck, maybe this is the most relaxed I've ever felt.

Eric's hands grip my hips, and then I'm being flipped onto my back and my hands are being lifted above my head when something smooth wraps around my wrists and attaches to the headboard.

I don't have time to react to that before goosebumps appear all over my skin from the cold, sticky liquid being traced around my nipple. I moan when I feel the warmth of Eric's mouth as his tongue traces where the liquid was.

Chocolate Sundae topping.

I thought I saw him grabbing it from the fridge but I wasn't sure.

All thought leaves me when he repeats the motion to the other nipple, then drips the sticky topping down my middle to my belly button and proceeds to follow it with his tongue, nipping and sucking at my waist and hips before licking and sucking it from my belly button.

"So sweet," he murmurs, continuing his onslaught further down, nipping at my inner thighs.

My hips buck when his tongue flicks over my clit. His eyes rise to mine, and I can only slightly make out the corners of his mouth lifting in a subtle smile right before he pushes two fingers inside me. I was so distracted by his tongue trailing my body that I have no idea when he got rid of my panties, but I'm not complaining.

My head falls back onto the pillow, and I'm pulling against the binds around my wrist as Eric continues his deliciously slow torture on my body. I want to run my fingers through his hair and grip it in my hands as I hold his face between my legs, urging him to make me come.

"Eric," I moan.

Nobody has ever made me feel like this, and I'm basking in it, but right now I need to come so freaking bad. I'm afraid if he doesn't let me come soon I might lose my mind.

"What do you want, baby?"

He moves from his position between my legs, losing his underwear, and ripping open a condom wrapper.

"You. I want you."

As soon as the words leave my lips he's pushing into me and releasing my hands from their binds. My legs move to wrap around his hips and I dig my fingers into his back through his shirt.

Like I knew I wouldn't, I don't last long before my body detonates, and I'm burying my face in his neck as I come hard. Eric soon follows behind me. I feel the muscles in his back stiffen and strain against my fingers and his sweaty shirt.

"So, you're not mad?" I grin up at him when we've both caught our breath enough to talk.

He chuckles, moving off me and disposing of the condom, then moving onto the bed and dragging my body back until I'm lying flush against him.

"I have no reason to be mad, A. I get it. I wasn't here, and you had to do what you had to do to move on. And you were able to handle things on your own. I'm not some caveman who thinks every woman needs a man to stand up for them and protect them. I know that if ever put into another situation like that, you'd have no problems protecting and standing up for yourself and anyone else. You never have."

I roll over and snuggle more into his chest, inhaling the scent of him and sex.

"I will say this though. Even though I know you can protect yourself and take on someone twice your size doesn't mean that I'm going to stand back and watch it happen. From now on, I have your back. Someone fucks with you, they fuck with me. You may not need anyone to fight your battles for you, but you can be damn certain I'll be there taking the hits for you."

"That goes both ways."

"Alice," he warns.

"No, no 'Alice.' If we're doing this then everything you just said about me goes for you too. Just because you're this tough, macho man, doesn't mean you have to go at it alone either. I don't care how hard, dangerous, or scary things get. I will always be right there with you, standing by your side, ready to take on whatever the world throws at us...with you. We've had fourteen years of going through this life alone, and without each other. Now we get to do it together."

Something akin to awe flashed behind his eyes, but when he shakes his head slightly and smiles it disappears. Eric pulls me in closer to his chest, and places a kiss on my forehead. "It's time for bed."

I don't argue with him, it was a long day and I'm exhausted, but if he thinks he can end this conversation there and I'll forget about it then he has another thing coming. I meant what I said, I have every intention on being right by his side through whatever is thrown our way. I'm not giving him up without a fight this time around.

Thirteen

Alice

"SO, WHEN ARE we going to meet Eric?" Kat nudges my arm as our server hands out another round of peach belinis.

I knew the question was coming. After all, I was the one who kept bugging them when they started dating the guys in our group, so it was only fair that the tables have now turned. Even though I knew it was coming, I was still unprepared to answer it.

I did want them to meet Eric, and I wanted Eric to get to know these women. But I liked the push and pull we had going on right now. If he meets two of the most important people in my life, it means it becomes real at that point. It means I have to believe he's home for good. I don't think I'm ready to accept that he is yet. Because if I do and he leaves again I'm not sure I would be able to stand it. Though, he swears he isn't leaving again.

Soon, was the only answer I'm willing to give them at this point.

"'Soon' isn't an answer, A." Dani levels me with a stare.

It's cute that she thinks she could give her version of a death glare at me and I'll crack, but it's not going to work. The only person who has been able to get away with using that tactic is Eric...and maybe my father.

Speaking of...

My phone rings, my dad's number, and a picture of my parents illuminated on the screen.

"Hi, Dad."

"Alice, your mom and I heard that Eric was back in town."

My dad, ladies and gentlemen, ever the one for pleasant greetings. *Note the hint of sarcasm.* I love my dad, I do. He's my rock in this shitty world, but sometimes I use to swear that he liked Eric more than he let on.

In the past, it was obvious he cared for him like a son, but he would never admit that letting Eric leave gutted him more than he allowed people to think. And I secretly think it hurt him, too, when Eric never came back like he said he would. I know my dad wishes he had done more to keep Eric in Oceanview, to raise him as part of our family, but at the time his hands were tied. Even still, I don't think my dad ever forgave himself for not doing more.

"He is." I sigh into the phone, narrowing my eyes at my two best girl friends sitting across from me doing everything in their power to stop giggling.

Why? Because they know now that my parents are aware of Eric's presence back in town they'll want me to bring him over. Which means that my mother will be extending an open invitation to my group of friends... Which means these two bitches will get to meet Eric.

I love them, I really *really* do, but they're dead for letting it slip to my mom that Eric was in town.

"Good. Your mother is wanting to throw a barbeque this weekend. Bring him with you, and she wants you to tell Dani to bring that apple crisp of hers we love so much."

My dad's voice is so deep that it comes out loud and clear through the speakers of the phone without it actually being on speaker, so Dani and Kat can hear every word he says which causes them to giggle hard.

I hate them. I watch enough detective and forensic shows that it would be easy for me to hide a body...or two. I rest my forehead in the palm of my hand and shake my head.

So much for keeping Eric to myself a little bit longer.

I assure my dad that we will all be there, and that Dani will have her apple crisp in hand before ending the call and glaring at the two giggling pain in the butts in front of me.

"You told my mom Eric was in town?"

Kat snorts, trying to wipe the smile off her face, and paste on a more serious look. Tries and fails, might I add.

"In our defense, we didn't know you hadn't told them he was back yet."

Fair enough, but, "When did you guys run into my mom?"

Kat looks over to Dani, a wide grin spreading across her face, and Dani sighs.

"At the hair salon. Bella was due for a much needed haircut, and Mom happened to be there at the same time."

"I call bullshit." I lean back against the leather of the booth and cross my arms under my chest.

Dani narrows her eyes at Kat before swinging her gaze over at me. Sometimes they forgot how well I'm able to read people. It's a gift or a curse, depends on the day, I guess.

"Fine," she huffs, a blush creeping up her neck. "At the timmies she always goes to."

I don't think my eyes could go any wider if I tried. "You sort her out?"

Kat shrugs, a smirk still on her face. "You weren't giving us anything, and Mom loves us so... we figured we'd show up and have coffee with her if she was there."

Dani nods, "I needed to talk about something... anything that didn't revolve around cartoons or homework or the latest video game craze. I love my family, but sometimes a woman just needs to..." she trails off looking for the right word.

"Live vicariously through her single friends," Kat finishes.

"Not quite." Dani giggles. "But close. I'll take it."

"You guys, I'm not that exciting. My life is pretty boring now that the two of you settled down."

"Yeah, but how's the sex?" Kat blurts and instantly turns a new shade of red.

"What are you talking about? Have you two seen your husbands?" I can't believe we're having this conversation right now. If anything, I should be asking them that question, not the other way around. Although, I'm not going to lie... sex with Eric is pretty fucking great.

Dani sighs, crossing her arms on the table. "Ever since Bella came to live with us full time, and now with this new pregnancy, Parker has been treating me like a delicate flower."

I choke and sputter on the bellini I just took a huge sip of. "A delicate flower?"

She shrugs. "I don't know how else to describe it. It's like he's afraid I'm going to break, when in reality all I want him to do is fuck me. Push me up against a wall and…"

My hands fly to my ears just as Dani finishes her sentence, while Kat nods along in agreement. I'm not a prude, I like sex. A lot. I do not, however, like picturing my best friends and their husbands going at it like bunnies.

"So yes, we want to live vicariously through you," Dani finishes when I remove my hands from my ears.

My eyes flicker between both of theirs, but all that stares back at me are serious faces. They're not fucking kidding. I pick up my check as soon as our waiter puts them down on the table and inch my way out of the booth.

"I love y'all, but no."

"Come on, Alice," Kat whines, even as a teasing grin spreads across her face.

"See you at Mom and Dad's this weekend." I wave over my shoulder as I make my way back through the dining room of the restaurant and out the heavy glass doors.

Fourteen

Alice

THE HOT WATER feels so good on my muscles. Between hitting the gym every other day this week and marathon sex with Eric, I had gotten more than my planned workouts. My lips thin in a smile when I hear the shower curtain squeak open behind me and then Eric's hands are on my hips.

"Someone's happy to see me." I push my ass back and wiggle just enough to cause his fingertips to curl into my hip.

"Baby, he's always happy to see you."

Giggling I turn around in his arms. My breath catches in my throat when I get a look at his chest. This is the first time I'm seeing him without a shirt on. Usually he keeps it on while we're having sex or he's taking me from behind. I can't help the shocked expression when I see there are scars and burns of varying lengths and thickness decorating his entire torso and parts of his upper arms.

"Alice."

My hand pauses halfway to his chest and when my eyes snap up to his there's pain swimming behind them.

"Who did this to you?" I choke out.

"Nobody you need to worry about."

Eric twitches slightly when I run a finger gently down one of the bigger scars. I don't know if the pain I saw in his eyes was from the memories of how these scars and burns came to be, or because it's what my eyes first landed on when I turned around.

"Alice…" His voice sounds hoarse when I lean forward and follow my fingers with soft kisses as they trace each scar on his upper chest. These scars and burns are a part of him, and as much as I hate knowing where they probably came from and who delivered them, they belong to the man who does and always has owned my heart.

My teeth pull slightly and graze over his earlobe right before I whisper, "Make love to me, Eric."

Before I even got the "me" part of my sentence out, he already has my back pressed against the shower tiles and my legs wrapped around his back. He slides into me while his mouth is placing drugging kisses along my collarbone and up my neck to that place behind my ear.

This.

I could get used to this. I could get used to spending my days and nights like this, in Eric's arms, with his cock filling my pussy. I could get used to waking up in the morning with him sleeping beside me, his dark hair all messed up. I could get used to walking into the kitchen for my morning cup of coffee and seeing him standing by the coffeemaker, shirtless…or naked. Either worked well for me.

As the walls of my pussy clench around him and my orgasm takes over, my nails rake over more scars on his back. It's all I can do to keep the tears from falling. I know he said to not cry for him, but I can't help it. This big, powerful man was put through so much in the years we were forced apart. I only wish I could erase the bad memories.

A sob manages to escape past my throat as my feet touch the shower floor again.

"Hey." He tips my chin up with his finger, his thumb running over my bottom lip. "Baby, please don't cry."

"W-Who would do this to you?" My fingers skim over the various scars again.

"Alice, baby. It's in the past. They can't touch me anymore."

"You said you were still dealing with it." I blink up at him, willing him to tell me it's over, and whatever he was *dealing* with is done.

"Alice." He throws open the shower curtain and steps out grabbing a towel and wrapping it around his waist. "I'm still working on it. But believe me when I tell you they can't touch me anymore."

"Eric." I follow him out of the bathroom wrapping my own towel around my body. "If it's the MC, how are you so sure they can't touch you? Or me, for that matter?"

Eric stops dead in his tracks. "What?"

"You said before that you stopped all contact with me because you were afraid of what they would do to me. What makes you so sure that after you've *dealt* with it they won't come after me to get to you?"

"Because I'd kill them."

"Eric…"

He steps towards me, his hands finding the sides of my face, "I'm serious, Alice. I'm done playing his game with his rules. If he so much as lays a hand on you I'd kill him"

"And then what? Spend the next twenty-five in prison? Eric, we've already lost fourteen years. I don't want to lose another twenty-five."

"We won't."

My eyebrow raises in question at his statement. "You sound so confident."

"I am." He grins. "They told me not to tell you what I'm about to divulge, but I need you to trust me, and to know that after this thing with the Knights' MC is done we can finally be together like we were supposed to ten years ago."

"Who's they?"

"The RCMP. More specifically, the ERT unit."

I'm pretty sure my eyes popped out of my head with what he said, but I couldn't be sure.

"You're working with Parker, Jay, and Mike?"

"And their teams. Cole and I met when I first moved out to Toronto. He's the one who introduced me to the guys, and the reason we've been able to set the ball in motion to take down the club."

"Drug trafficking…" I whisper mostly to myself but it doesn't go unnoticed by Eric.

"What?"

"My friend, Dani, mentioned that the guys had caught a drug trafficking case. Is that the one that involves the club?"

He nods, still peering down at me. "Look, A. When things go down promise me you and the girls will take a trip somewhere, that you won't be in town, or anywhere close to here."

"Why?"

"Promise me, Alice," he pleads.

"Why, Eric?" I push.

"Jesus, woman. Do you have to ask so many questions? Why can't you just do as I ask?"

Putting my hands on my hips, I put on my best *fuck you* look and stare him down. His resolve slowly crumbles when he sits on the edge of the bed, leans his elbows on his knees, and intertwines his fingers. The pose makes his arms look even bigger.

Focus, Alice! You can ogle him later.

"I need you to make sure you're nowhere near this city when the club comes to town, because if they see that there's a connection between us they'll have no qualms about taking you too. If the plan doesn't work."

"Taking me?"

"Selling you, Alice. It's not just drugs they're trafficking. Fuck, knowing how messed up my father and his VP are, they'll probably keep you for themselves."

My breath leaves me in one foul whoosh when I sit down on the edge of the bed next to him. "If the plan doesn't work," I repeat back to him in a daze, my eyes unfocused and staring ahead at the wall.

"Baby, look at me." Eric places his hands on my shoulders and tries to turn my body to face him but my eyes are still staring at the wall ahead. I'm not seeing the wall. Instead, my brain is playing the multiple ways that things could go wrong. He could die; they could kill him. "Alice, look at me." There's more demand in his voice this time.

Slowly, my eyes scan the side of the room until they find his dark eyes leveled at me in concern.

"That's not going to happen, okay? I won't let them touch you. I'll kill every last one of them before I'd allow them to touch one hair on your head. They've already stolen fourteen years from us. I won't allow them to steal more."

"What exactly does this plan entail?"

He sighs dropping his hands from my shoulders. "Get dressed. I'll make a call and see if I can get the guys over here to help explain it to you."

Fifteen

ERIC

"**YOU WANT HIM** to do what?!" Alice shrieks after Parker finishes telling her the plan to take down my dad and his club.

If I wasn't so worried about making sure she was nowhere near this city when they came to town I would find her outburst hot. Nobody has ever cared about me like she does, except for my brother Brad.

Even when we were kids, Alice was always standing up for me when no one would. She went up against the biggest bully in our elementary school because he stole my glasses for fuck's sake.

I wasn't completely honest with her before. Yes, I want her out of town because I am afraid of what the club would do to her if they found out who she was to me. But I was even more afraid of what she would do to my dad and his VP for causing the scars that decorate my chest and back.

I was afraid that given half the chance she would stand against my father, the president of an MC, and she would mostly likely fucking win. I don't think this woman has a fear-ridden bone in her body. She doesn't give a rat's ass who somebody is, she'll go toe-to-toe with them if they mess with someone she cares about. Heck, she could make any grown ass man quiver in his boots. Kind of like she was doing to Parker at this very minute with that perfected death glare.

"Alice, we have all the bases covered. We'll have snipers on the roof and a team on the water."

I lower my chin to my chest and try to hide the grin that has appeared on my face. Parker sounds like he's trying to soothe a child. If he's trying to reassure her that everything will go smoothly, that's not going to work on Alice.

"She's about to let him have it, isn't she?" Cole whispers next to me.

As the words leave his mouth, Alice's back straightens, her arms cross over her chest, and her face morphs into a deep scowl. God, my girl is sexy as fuck when she's gearing up for a fight. The skin-tight skirt and fuck me boots only add to the sex appeal.

Right when I think she's going to rip him a new one, she surprises the fuck out of me and her shoulders relax as she takes a deep breath and exhales. "And you'll have his back?"

What the fuck? What was with the three-sixty? Not that I'm not grateful she's starting to see the necessity of the situation, but a second ago she was ready to tear into Parker like a Pitbull.

Parker nods. "You have my word that we'll have his back. Four of us will be on the ground within range of him at all times."

Alice's gaze swings over to mine from across the room before she turns back to Parker. "Okay then."

"What just happened?" Cole asks, keeping his voice low.

"I have no fucking clue," I reply, but I have feeling the other shoe is about to drop.

"When's the club due in town?"

It takes me a little while to realize everyone is looking at me, and waiting for a reply. I slip my cell out of my pants pocket and double check the day they're arriving.

"The shipment arrives a week from today. They'll be here the day before."

"So, Alice and the girls will need to leave for their vacation a few days prior to that," Jay chimes in.

"My parents are giving us their beach house in White Rock for the week, and my mom has agreed to go down and help with the kids," Parker adds.

"I'm not leaving," Alice states, planting her hands firmly back on her hips.

And…there it is. The other shoe.

"Alice," I growl, stalking towards her.

This no fear act of hers isn't going to work on me. She can stand there and stare me down all day if she pleases, but she'll be going on that vacation with Dani and Kat, even if I'm the one who has to put her on that plane or in that car. She's going. There'll be no ands, ifs, or buts about it. When the club comes roaring into town, Alice will not be here.

When I get within inches of her, I can hear her whimper from the growl in my voice, but she's determined to not allow it to shake her resolve to stay.

"Bedroom." My voice is low, but no less demanding.

She's almost panting. My girl may be fearless, but she likes it when I assert my dominance in the bedroom.

"Eric." The hands on her hips falter a split second and her voice comes out all breathy.

"Bedroom, Alice," I say low enough so that only her ears pick up my words.

A fire ignites behind her eyes, but she doesn't say anything in response as she turns and saunters off to her bedroom down the hall.

"I need to have a word with my girl," I say over my shoulder to the guys as I follow her. I hear Mark and Cole snicker behind me, and Mike saying something to the team, but I'm too far to catch it.

"Eric, I'm not…"

Her words are cut off when my lips crash down on hers and I suck her tongue into my mouth. We both groan. She tastes so fucking good, like sweet wine. I back her into the far wall of her bedroom until she's pressed firmly against it.

"You're going to White Rock." My teeth nip down her neck and collarbone.

"I'm not leaving you," she pants, digging her nails into my ribs.

My lips find hers again in a kiss that's more possessive than any we've shared so far. When I pull away her lips are swollen, and her breasts are heaving with each breath. She looks so damn hot right now, and if it weren't for the guys just down the hall, I would fuck her senseless right against this wall. Hell, maybe I will anyway.

"Baby, if anything happened to you I wouldn't be able to forgive myself. Please, just go with the girls. I won't be able to do my job if I'm constantly worrying about where you are. I promise I will call you as soon as it's safe for you to come home," I plead, staring into her intense eyes.

Her hands move from my waist to my face, and caress the light stubble that has grown. "Okay. I'll go. But promise me something." Her dark eyes are brimming with unshed tears as she looks up at me. "Promise me that when I come home I won't be coming home to a corpse. Promise me that you'll do everything possible to stay alive. I recently got you back, Eric. I'm not ready to lose you again."

I plant soft kisses on either side of her lips. "You won't lose me again."

"Good," she grins. "Now, get rid of the guys so we can go have dinner, and then you can bring me back here and finish what you started against this wall." Her lips slowly curl up into another grin as her teeth graze over her bottom lip.

I groan. "You know what that does to me."

"Oh, I know." She lowers her voice when one hand cups my cock through my jeans and squeezes. "I'm hoping that if I do it enough, we can hurry through dinner. I'm dying to feel this rock-hard cock in my pussy. I want you to fuck me until I can't stand anymore."

A growl rumbles through my chest when I press my hips into hers, a hand finding one of her nipples and tugging until a whimper passes her lips. "And if I say to hell with dinner, and fuck you right here? Right now."

She's not wasting any time when her fingers start fumbling with the button and zipper on my pants, yanking them and my underwear down in one.

I groan when my hand moves up a smooth thigh and finds nothing separating me from that pussy of hers. Alice leans back against the wall and pushes her hips forward, grinding her pussy against my hand. Small mewls escaping her throat as I thrust two fingers inside her wet heat.

My fingers curl under her backside. As soon as I lift her, her legs are wrapping around my hips, and I'm slamming into her, using the wall to keep her up when I remove one of my hands to tug down her shirt and free her breasts.

She groans digging her nails into my shoulders when I lick one of her nipples. When I tug it slightly with my teeth, her hips buck wildly. I grin and do it to the other one, causing the same reaction from her.

"Mmm, someone loves having her nipples tugged. Maybe we should try some nipple clamps next time."

"Oh, fuck yeah," she pants, pushing her breasts more towards my mouth.

As another moan leaves her sexy mouth, there's a knock at the door. Are you fucking kidding me? I'm about to make my girl come the hardest she's had yet, and we get interrupted.

"Yo! Eric, Parker wants to go over the plan one more time," Mike's voice sounds from the other side of the door.

"Not now, asshole."

I'm trying to keep my voice level and control my temper. When I look at Alice, there's a mischievous smirk on her face when one of her hands leaves my shoulder and trails down to rub her clit. *Well, I'll be damned.* Seems Ms. Alice Johnson likes the idea of almost being caught with her skirt up.

Alice's head falls back against the wall and her face contorts in pleasure when I slide out and slam back into her, with Mike still banging on the door. And she's biting on that damn lip again, albeit this time to keep herself from screaming out with each of my thrusts.

"Knight!" Mike calls again.

"Fuck off! Give me a damn second," I yell over my shoulder.

Just as we hear Mike move away from the door, the walls of her pussy clench, and her mouth rounds in a silent scream as she comes around my cock.

Fuck, she's beautiful.

Sixteen

ERIC

PREZ: *SHIPMENT ARRIVES in 7 days. Grim will be there in 5.*

Grim is the club's Sergeant at Arms, and the man my dad sends to do all his dirty work. He was known through all the chapters as the Grim Reaper. They called him the Grim Reaper because if he showed up at your place you were a dead man.

You know you fucked up when Dad sent Grim to have a *talk* with you. I scoff, yeah, a talk that more than likely ended torture and being chopped into pieces. If Grim was sent after you, nobody would ever find your body, and you could be damn sure he made you beg for death.

And he'd be on his way here in another five days. Plenty of time for me to get Alice, Kat, and Dani and her kids out of town. If Alice would fucking cooperate and leave like she was told.

"What's the word?" Parker crosses his arms and widens his stance. It's an act to reassert his dominance in the group. To make sure I know that while I've been given the chance to be vocal about how the takedown goes, he's still the one in charge.

"They're sending someone down in five days." I pocket my phone, my eyes finding Alice's across the room.

It looks like she's in a heated conversation with Kat and Dani. I'm hoping if I fail to talk her into leaving town that hearing it from those women will convince her it isn't safe. Alice shifts her weight from foot to foot, a tell that she's over the conversation, when her dark eyes look over Kat's shoulder and connect with mine.

She doesn't wait for the girls to finish their conversation before she's pushing past them and heading my way, fiery determination in her eyes.

I look from her to Parker, who tips his chin once, and suddenly everyone has filed out of the room, leaving Alice and I alone.

"I'm not going," she states, her hands on her hips.

"Alice," I groan. "This conversation is over. You're going. End of story."

That fiery determination turns to a boiling rage as she straightens her back and gets right up into my face, poking a finger into my chest.

"No. It's not 'end of story'."

Grabbing the hand with the finger poking me I pull her into my chest and spin, pushing her back up against the wall and using my knee to push her legs apart, my hips pining her into place.

"Babe, maybe I haven't made myself clear." I nip at her jaw and tug on her bottom lip. "You're going. Even if I have to pick your sexy ass up and put you in that car myself."

She's panting right now, little mews leaving those luscious lips as I lick down her neck. Her hands try to find purchase on my belt buckle but before they can get it undone I'm pinning both of them above her head. As much as I want to slide into her heat right now, I don't want to fuck my woman with an audience. But that doesn't mean I'm not going to rile her up the rest of the night until she's begging me to fuck her.

Gripping both of her wrists in my one hand and freeing the other, I let it roam up the inside of her thighs 'til it reaches her hot center.

"Fuck, baby, still no panties?"

She grins, tugging her bottom lip between her teeth. And I lose it. Her head thumps back against the wall and her back arches as I thrust two fingers inside her pussy.

"Don't come," I instruct, finding her swollen clit with my thumb.

"Eric," she moans, her breaths coming faster.

"Do not come, Alice."

When I know she's hovering on the verge of an orgasm, I withdraw my fingers, move them to her lips and watch as she slowly flicks her tongue over them before pulling them into her mouth and sucking her juices from them. My cock hardens even more at the sight.

"Let's go get dinner before I change my mind and fuck you right here and now where everyone can hear you scream my name."

✳✳✳

ALICE

My pulse is racing and my breaths are coming in short bursts as Eric releases my hands and pushes away. Part of me wants to say fuck it, grab him by the front of his shirt and press my body to his, pleading for him to take me against this wall.

The other part of me doesn't want to share our private moments with our friends. Doing it in public has always had an appeal to me. The thought of being caught on the verge of an orgasm only he could deliver, his rock-hard cock in my wet pussy…yeah, there was something about almost getting caught that sent heat racing through my body.

When we pull up to the restaurant, Eric gets out and runs to my side, opening the door and reaching in to help me out. I was surprised when he walked out of the room dressed in dark jeans, a button-down shirt, and a black suit jacket.

In all the years' I had known him, he hated dressing up. Despised it, actually. I wasn't going to lie though, he looked damn hot. I smiled knowing that he was all mine, and slid my hand in his.

It wasn't hard for us to slip back into old ways, like we hadn't been apart for so many years. The inside jokes, the nights spent at our spot at the lake talking about anything and everything. It all came back like nothing had changed.

But it had.

Life had changed both of us. There was a darkness in both of us that hadn't been there before. His from years of abuse at the hands of the club, and mine from learning more about my family's history. I hid it well though. Nobody knew, especially Eric.

I look around the dimly lit restaurant, a small smile tugging at my lips of the memories from the first time Eric brought me here.

It was my fifteenth birthday. I was adamant that I didn't want to do anything for it, mostly because most of our friends had forgotten it was my birthday, and I was feeling bummed. So, he made me get dressed up and brought me here for dinner. When I found out where we were going I told him I thought it was too expensive and I would've been okay to just go watch a movie but he insisted it wasn't too expensive. He had gotten paid from his lawn mowing job and wanted to treat me for my day. But I knew he had been saving up for months.

Like tonight, the night he brought me here also happened to be the same night they had live music. We stuffed ourselves full of pasta and then danced. It was my first dance, and the first time I started having feelings toward him. He had been my best friend since we were three. But that night stirred something in me.

The band takes a little break and when they come back they start playing a cover of a song I know all too well. It was the same song we danced to all those years ago. *When You Say Nothing at All* by Boyzone still caused my heart to flutter like it did that night.

Eric grins, places his fork back down on his plate, and wipes his mouth on the napkin before reaching out for my hand and pulling me onto the dance floor with him.

He spins me before pulling me into him, gripping my right hand in his and placing his left hand at the small of my back.

"Remember this song?" he asks, his lips brushing my ear.

"How could I forget."

"The smile on your face lets me know that you need me. There's a truth in your eyes sayin' you'll never leave me. The touch of your hand says you'll catch me if ever I fall. You say it best when you say nothing at all," he softly sings in my ear, and I melt into him, allowing myself to fall a little more in love with him.

Love.

I've known for a long time that I love him. He was, and always will be, the only man for me. When he was gone, it felt like a big part of me was missing. Nothing ever felt quite right without him. And now I felt whole again. That part of me was no longer missing.

It was always him, and it will always be him.

But I had yet to tell *him* that. I was stubborn too though. I knew he felt the same way, so I am determined to wait until he says it first. I have no idea why, since I am a take-charge type of person, and couldn't give two shits about doing things the 'traditional' way.

But this, this falling in love with my best friend, of possibly getting my heart broken again like only Eric could break it, this scared the shit out of me. I needed to know he felt the same way before I tell him how I feel and make myself vulnerable to him again.

"Let's get out of here," he whispers, trailing kisses up my neck.

I nod and go to gather my purse and his jacket while he pays our bill.

Seventeen

ERIC

A S WE'RE WALKING out of the restaurant I immediately spot Grim on his bike in the shadows. I hope Alice doesn't notice that I've picked up our pace to get her back into her car before Grim decides to get off his bike and approach us. But in true Alice fashion, nothing gets past her.

"Who's that?"

"No one. Let's go." I put more pressure on her lower back and try to keep her moving.

"Eric, I'm not some fragile girl. Tell me. That's him, isn't it? Grim?" She looks over her shoulder while I'm still trying to move her toward her car.

"Yes." I unlock and open her door trying to urge her to get in but she stops and look over the door behind me at Grim who has now swung his leg over his bike.

I can hear my heart start to race in my ears. *Fuck, she can't still be here when he comes over.*

"Alice, please." I try to communicate everything to her in the way I look at her and in the kiss I placed on her soft lips. "Get in the car and go. I'll come by later."

"Eric..." she pleads as I hear Grim's boots get closer.

"Go, Alice." I put as much venom as I can in my voice without scaring her but I need her to go. Now.

Finally, she nods and gets in the car, closing and locking the door as she starts the engine and takes off. Thank God. Now that she's not here I can concentrate on figuring out why he's here five days early, and convincing him I've been doing my job while down here.

Taking a deep breath and squaring my shoulders, I turn to face him. "Grim, what are you--"

I don't get to finish my sentence before Grim hits me with an upper cut to my stomach. Holy shit, this guy has knuckles of steel.

"Your dad says hello." His voice is cold with each word, and then the world goes black.

***

ALICE

I know Eric told me to go home and wait for him there but I can't bring myself to leave him behind. So I do the only thing I can think of. Shoot off a S.O.S messages to Jay and Parker, and then hightail it back to the restaurant.

I get back in time to see the Knight's MC Sergeant at Arms haul Eric's limp body over his shoulder and stuff him into the trunk of a nearby car. Once the trunk is closed he taps on the top and the car takes off while he jumps back on his bike and follows behind them.

Once I think they're a safe distance ahead I slowly pull out of my parking spot and follow behind them. My phone rings and when I don't answer, it pings with several messages but I ignore them all.

Parker: *Do not go back to the restaurant.*
Parker: *Alice?!*
Parker: *For fuck's sake Alice! Answer your phone!*
Jay: *Stay out of sight. We're on our way.*

It doesn't surprise me that the guys already know where they're headed with Eric. They probably had some sort of tracker on his phone from the beginning, and right now I'm thankful for that.

***

ERIC

My head feels heavy and my arms feel like they're burning when I start coming to. I realize why when I try to bring my arms down but they get pulled right back up again and I hear the rustling of chains.

"It's about time you woke up. I was starting to get bored."

"Grim? What the fuck?! Let me down, you fucker."

He chuckles, wheeling a metal cart in front of him and placing it just out of my field of vision. My stomach falls. I've gone on plenty of calls with Grim to know what the metal cart means, and exactly which tools he loves to use. The push pick in particular is one he always gravitates toward.

"You know, Eric, I never did like you, but you were the Prez's son. But now…" He lifts the ice pick from the cart and examines it in the little bit of light streaming through the lone window. "Now, you're nothing. As soon as the Prez found out what you were really doing down here he gave the go ahead to have a talk with you."

There's a gleam in the sonofabitch's eyes when he looks from the pick to me. The fucker gets off on this, torturing people until they're begging for death. By the time he's through with them they've given up all hope of begging him to spare their lives and they start begging for death. Begging him to put them out of their misery. Grim is one sick fuck, and now all his efforts were focused on me.

Blinding hot pain shoots through me as he pushes the pick through my sternum.

Fuck, that kills.

Grim pulls it free, only to push it in again between my ribs, and again lower down. My head falls back between my shoulder blades and my eyes shut against the pain but I still refuse to give him the satisfaction of screaming out in pain.

He continues his stabbing assault on my torso until there are as many fresh wounds as there are scars of old ones. I can feel myself getting weak from all the blood loss, but I try to hold on. I need to make it out of here and to Alice. I promised her I wouldn't leave her again, and I intend to make good on that promise.

Grim walks over to the metal cart and replaces the push pick with a scalpel. Where the hell he managed to acquire that from, I have no idea. But shit's about to get real, because the one he's holding in his hand is the exact same one surgeons use to open someone up.

My breath starts coming in quick puffs as I prepare myself for whatever he has planned for me next.

"You know, I might have to take that sweet thing for myself. Once you're dead she's going to need someone to care for her." He grabs the front of his pants, licking his lips. "She looks like she'll be a lot of fun. Tell me, Eric. Is she a fighter?" He smirks.

"You sonofabitch, stay away from her! I'll kill you," I hiss, fighting to stay conscious so I can get out of these chains, but they have no fucking give in them.

His phone ringing has Grim putting the scalpel down and turning away from me so that I can't hear his conversation. The only thing I catch is him saying, "Okay, boss." Before pocketing the phone and turning back to me, pulling the firearm from the waistband of his jeans behind his back.

"Hate to cut this little talk short but the Prez says I have to get it done. Oh, and don't you worry about that sweet piece of ass. I'll make sure to take *real* good care of her," he sneers, then pulls the trigger.

Eighteen

Alice

I KNOW I should've listening to Jay and stayed out of sight but as soon as I heard the gunshot and saw Grim exit the warehouse with Eric nowhere in sight I didn't think, I just reacted. My man was in there, possibly hurt, and he needed me.

The next thing I know, my feet led me to where Eric was hanging, strung by his wrists, his feet barely touching the floor. Luckily, it was on a pulley system, so all I had to do was lower it down until I was able to undo the chains binding his wrists together.

"Don't you fucking die on me, Eric!"

I'm frantically trying to put as much pressure as I can on the bullet wound in his chest but there's so much blood. I'm not even sure if my hands are covering where it entered his flesh. Or if the bullet wound is the source of all the blood. It could be any number of the stab wounds decorating his chest and limbs.

"You're not allowed to leave me now, you sonuvabitch! I just got you back," I sob. "Don't leave me…" my voice comes out as a whisper. "You promised…"

Eric's head lolls to the side and his eyes lock on mine. His hand comes up to cup my face before his entire body goes limp. It was like for that spilt second, he wanted to memorize the way I looked as I saw his life start slipping away.

"No," my voice croaks as I hear running feet behind me. "Eric!" My breaths are coming fast, and I'm no longer concerned about putting pressure on his wound as my hands fly up to his face, framing it. My hands are covered in blood.

His blood.

But I don't care right now. He can't be dead.

He can't be.

He promised we'd be able to really be together after this. After having lost him for fourteen years, he was finally going to be mine, and I his.

"I love you," I whisper in his ear, hoping that by finally coming clean about how I feel he'll hold onto that and fight for his life. But nothing changes, he's still lying under me...lifeless.

"Alice!" Parker, Jay, and Cole's voices sound behind me.

"You have to move, A, so we can help him," Mike's arms wrap around me and drag me away from Eric's still body.

When he turns and hands me over to Parker my fists start flying. "You said he wouldn't get hurt! You fucking said you'd have his back!" I'm pounding into his chest but Parker held me until all the fight leaves me.

Parker lifts his head to Mike. I already know we lost him but hearing Parker curse and feeling his arms wrap more securely around me is my undoing.

Feeling like a big part of myself died alongside Eric, I collapse in Parker's arms. Eric's been my best friend since we were kids. Yes, we had lost touch for so many years, but our friendship was like those where it didn't matter how long you went without talking or seeing each other, when you cross paths again you could pick up right where you left off. That's what it was like with us. It felt like no time at all had passed. And now he was gone.

***

After leaving the dock, Parker took me home and tried to apologize again, and make sure that I was okay, but I barely heard a word he said as I headed towards my bedroom where Eric's smell still lingered, and burrowed under the sheets that smelt of him.

The next few days went by in a blur. When people called I ignored all their calls, when they knocked I ignored that, too. I know I should've probably been helping Brad plan his brother's funeral, but I couldn't bring myself to leave the bed that held the smell, and so many memories of being curled up in his arms, feeling his fingers on my skin, his breath on my cheek, his lips on mine. My nose and throat burn from all the tears I've shed over the last several days.

But his scent was fading from his pillow, and I knew it was only a matter of time before one of the guys had had enough and broke into my house, if I didn't move my ass. I didn't care though. I was afraid that if I didn't savour what was left of him, I would forget. I was scared that despite all the years we spent together, I would forget the memories--his smell, his voice, the feel of his body wrapped around mine. I wanted to live in the memories of the last couple months a little longer. I should have told him I loved him when I had the chance. It would be the biggest regret of my life, knowing I missed my chance.

The sheets are suddenly ripped off me. When my eyes snap open Brad is staring down at me, frustration clouding his dark irises.

"Get your ass up, A."

"Fuck off, Brad." I try to turn over and give him my back, but strong hands grip my hips and hurl me out of bed and over his shoulder. I don't remember when he got into town, but then again I don't remember much of the last few days. "What the fuck. Put me down!"

He walks me into my bathroom and deposits me into the shower before turning the cold water on.

"What's your problem, asshole?" I glare at him after turning the hot water up.

"You're not the only one who lost him," he growls. "Get cleaned up and come out to the kitchen. I'll have dinner ready."

He storms off, slamming the bathroom door behind him, leaving me under the now warm water of the shower. I forgot how alike Eric and Brad were. They were both demanding, but fiercely protective over those they held dear.

They looked alike too.

Lots of people usually mistook them for being twins, despite Brad being ten years older, and a month away from his fortieth birthday. They both had dark as night hair that they wore slightly longer, and both had chocolate-brown eyes that turned midnight when they were angry. But the difference was that Brad was still here, while Eric was taken from me. Us.

"Okay, I'm dressed," I say, walking into the kitchen, pulling my tank top the rest of the way down my stomach. When I look at Brad, something flashes in his eyes, but it's gone before I can decipher what it is. "Now, what do you want?" He tracks my every moment when I move to take a seat at the breakfast bar.

"You're helping me plan the funeral," he states while placing steaks and roasted potatoes and vegetables on each of the two plates in front of him.

Brad pushes one of the plates towards me, before turning back to the fridge and retrieving an already chilled and poured glass of white wine and setting it on the bar next to my plate. My eyebrows raise in question at the way he just made himself at home in my kitchen. Nobody has cooked for me in here before, except for Eric.

"Eat," he instructs. Bossy as always.

"Thought you would've already taken care of it," I say, popping the newly cut piece of steak in my mouth. Oh, my lanta, this guy can cook. I close my eyes and a small moan escapes as the spices hit my tastebuds. It's cooked perfectly. Medium rare. I don't eat a lot of meat, but steak is one of my weaknesses.

A throat clearing pulls me out of my thoughts, and when I open my eyes Brad has his arms braced on the bar on either side of his plate and his head bent.

"You okay?"

"Fine," he grunts, cutting another piece of his steak. "You're the only other person who knows what Eric would've wanted. I need your help with this, A. My mother is worthless, and I don't want my father and his club anywhere near the funeral."

I sputter and cough on the sip of wine, turning to him with eyes wide. "You knew?"

His shoulders square, but he doesn't turn to face me. "Of course I knew. I wasn't about to let my brother go live with a practical stranger."

"You bastard!" I spit. "Do you have any idea what they did to him? You could've stopped it, Brad! You could've fought the court to have him stay with you."

This time he does level his gaze on me, and it takes every piece of strength I have to not cower in the corner like a fucking girl.

"You don't think I tried that? Damn it, Alice! I tried, but they didn't want to hear it. It didn't matter to them that I was twenty-five and had a successful career making more than enough to support the both of us. None of it fucking mattered."

"What are you saying, Brad?"

"I'm saying my father dearest either had someone threaten the judge or he was on his payroll. I was going to be denied custody of Eric before I even stepped foot in that damn courtroom."

"Well, you should've tried harder!" I yell, pushing out of my seat and pacing behind Brad. Forcing him to turn around.

"I was doing well for myself, but I didn't have the type of money it would've taken to go up against the MC."

"Still, there must've been something more you could've done!"

"Alice," Brad warned.

I spin on my heels. "They tortured him, Brad. You didn't see the scars and burns on his body. Your dad did that to him, and you could've prevented it!"

My fists shoot out to punch his chest but Brad catches my wrists in his hands and pulls me towards him. "Enough!"

I can't hold back the sobs that rack my body anymore. "He's gone, and your dad had him killed."

His hands leave my wrists and curl around me, pulling me more securely into him. "I'm sorry, baby girl."

There's nothing more for us to say. He holds me and lends his quiet strength to me while I break in his arms. I don't know if it's more reassuring or if it's lending towards my breakdown that his arms almost feel exactly like Eric's did when he wrapped them around me.

And then Brad is pushing me away, holding me at arm's length as he peers down at me. "What do you mean my dad had him killed?"

"We were just leaving the restaurant after a date when Grim showed up out of nowhere. Eric made me get in the car and leave without him before Grim got off his bike. I got about two blocks away before I turned around and went back, but by that time he had Eric loaded in the trunk of a car. I followed them to a warehouse on the dock, and when I heard the gunshots and saw Grim walk back out and get on his bike. I knew Eric was in trouble, so I went in and found him hanging by his wrists, and bleeding out."

"Fuck. Dad sent the club Sergeant at Arms after his own son?"

"You really have no idea what's going on, do you?" I ask, raising an eyebrow and crossing my arms.

Brad drops his head, running a hand through his perfectly styled hair. "I tried keeping up to date on Eric's life and my dad's club as much as I could, but a few years ago I lost communication with my contact."

"Contact? What contact?"

"I can't tell you that."

"What the hell are you messed up in, Brad?"

"Nothing. Look, Alice, just tell me what the hell has been going on."

Sighing, I walk around the counter and grab the bottle of whiskey I keep on hand in cases of emergency, in the cupboard on top of the fridge. This definitely counted as an emergency. I was about to relive all the pain of the memories Eric had confided in me, and it was going to suck.

"You might want to take a seat and get comfy. This may take awhile." I grabbed two glass tumblers and poured a few fingers worth of whiskey in each.

Brad settles in on the other side of the breakfast bar and I lean against the counter as I recount everything I've been told about the club's business. From the usual drug trafficking, to human trafficking, and the raping of the women and children who come in the shipping containers every month. As well as all the torture the club put Eric through when he first arrived there, and how all the scars came to be on his body. I tell him the original plan to ambush the club after the next shipment arrived, but how Grim had shown up five days early.

"And you know what happened after that."

I hand Brad the bottle and sink deeper into the couch. Halfway through my recount of everything I had been told we ditched the glasses, moved to the couch, and started doing shots straight from the bottle.

He doesn't take a drink, instead leans forward with his elbows on his knees and the almost empty bottle of JD dangling between his fingers, a faraway look in his eyes.

"I fucked up."

If I hadn't been looking at him in this moment, I would've missed what he said. I'm almost certain I wasn't supposed to catch on to the words leaving his mouth and that they were meant for his benefit alone.

"How?" I ask, afraid of the answer.

Brad takes a swig of the amber liquid then balancing the bottle on his leg with a couple fingers settles into the back of the couch, leaning his head back.

"I should've known something was up when I couldn't get a hold of my contact. If I had bothered to look into his disappearance more maybe I could've still had eyes on Eric. I could've prevented his death."

"That's crazy."

"No." He shook his head before taking another swig from the bottle.

"You of all people should know that once your dad decides he wants something, nothing short of death is going to stop him. He would've found another way."

The sound of glass crashing against the fireplace makes me jump in my seat and my eyes to shut against Brad's yelling. I don't say anything, let him continue yelling and getting it out. He's hurting, and if this is the only way for him to come to terms with that then he can yell as much as he wants. I'm hurting too, the love of my life was taken away from me, and I hadn't told him how much he meant to me. Maybe Brad and I could hurt together, and maybe, just maybe we could heal together too.

When it's been quiet for some time, I take a deep cleansing breath and let it out before slowly opening my eyes. When I do, the scene in front of me breaks my heart a little more. Brad is sitting on the edge of the couch, bent over with his head in his hands, his back heaving. He's the toughest guy I know, and he's breaking apart right in front of my eyes.

He tenses beneath my touch when I place a hand on his shoulder.

"I shouldn't have lost my shit like that. I'm sorry."

"It's okay. Sometimes we need to lose our shit."

New sobs rack his body. "Eric was the only thing I had in this fucked up world. He was my baby brother, and I should've looked out for him."

I wrap both my arms around him and hold him while he mourns the lost of the only real family member he had.

"I'll kill them. Every last one of them. I'll kill them for what they did to him."

I didn't doubt it either. Brad was huge. Even growing up, nobody dared mess with him because they knew he would fuck them up. That, coupled with the need he felt to avenge his brother's death, and his temper. It was a deadly combination. I hoped he didn't get himself killed in the process. He was my only connection to Eric, and as selfish as it may seem now, I wasn't about to lose him, too.

Nineteen

I REFUSED TO talk to any of the guys after Eric died. I know it isn't fair to them. Anything could've gone down that night. But they promised me they would have his back.

They fucking promised.

Now instead of being curled up in his arms where I belonged, and telling him how much I loved him. I had planned his funeral with Brad.

"You ready, honey?" My mom's knuckles rap on my childhood bedroom door.

I couldn't stomach going back to my house after Brad showed up and dragged my ass out of bed. There were too many memories of Eric there. A slow, sad smile pulls at the corner of my mouth when I meet my mother's eyes from the mirror standing in front of me. Tears pooled in my honey-brown eyes.

"Here, let me help you with that," she says, taking the delicate chain from my fingers and securing it around my neck when I lift my hair.

"Beautiful." Her hands linger on my shoulders for a second longer before she takes a step back.

"Ready?" my dad asks, appearing in the doorway to my room as he pulls on the cuffs of his dark suit then comes to stand beside my mom.

My heart tugs painfully at the sight of them. They look so perfect together. He always has a smile on his face whenever she's near. As a kid when I pictured my future relationships, I would picture theirs. My dad grounds my mom, and my mom makes him lighter, kind of like Eric and me.

Those tears that were pooling in my eyes are now running down my cheeks. My dad silently opens his arms and I don't hesitate to walk into them, allowing myself the small reprieve his arms have always provided. I'm glad I decided to forgo the makeup and mascara.

"Come on, the sooner we go do this, the sooner I can bring you back here and we can curl up on the couch with pints of ice cream." When he speaks I can feel his voice rumble through his chest.

I was a daddy's girl through and through. According to Mom, when I was a baby I would refuse to sleep until my dad would swoop me up and lay me down on his chest. He would quietly sing to me until I fell asleep, which usually resulted in him falling asleep as well. As I got older, I sought comfort in his arms.

Eventually he stopped asking me what was wrong when I came home in tears, he would open his arms and hold me for however long it took for me to be okay again. The morning Eric left for Ontario, Dad signed me out of school. We went to the range to fire off a few rounds, and then we hiked until we couldn't hike anymore. The next day we loaded our bikes into his truck and went to Whistler for a weekend of downhill mountain biking. He never forced me to talk about what it was I was feeling, and I never told him. He allowed me sometime away from it all while still keeping an eye on me to make sure I didn't do something stupid. After we got back and I had exhausted myself with every favorite physical activity, Mom took me for some retail therapy.

They were a great team, somehow always knowing what I need before I do.

"Ice cream on the couch sounds like a great idea." Mom gently places her hand on my back in a reassuring gesture.

I pull away from my dad's arms and nod, wiping away the tears with the pads of my fingers. I'm sure they won't be the last ones to fall today.

***

The funeral was a great tribute to the kind of man Eric was. But I was surprised when his dad and his MC brothers showed up.

I was not expecting that, and Brad had to hold me back from marching over to them and ripping them a new one. There were times throughout that I had to do the same for him. I know it angered him to no end that he couldn't confront them head on, but we had to be smart about it. I knew Parker and the teams still had a plan in place to bring the MC down, so Brad and I agreed we could let them do their thing, for now. But I didn't know how much longer I could hold him back. We both needed answers, and we both wanted to see the ones responsible for Eric's death rot in hell.

But what I was expecting, and completely not surprised about, was the fact that his mom didn't bother to show her face at her son's funeral.

"Thanks for helping me with this, A." Brad pulled me into a hug after everyone had given their condolences.

"You don't have to thank me, Brad. I would've done it anyway. I loved him."

"He loved you too, Alice. Ever since that day at the park."

I giggle. "We were three."

He shrugs, slipping one hand into the pocket of his suit pants. "He loved you his entire life. You were it for him."

Brad wipes away the tear that managed to escape its way down my cheek, places a soft kiss on my head, then turns and walks away.

I'm not entirely sure what just happened, but I pray he doesn't decide to take things into his own hands after all. I already lost one Knight brother, I wouldn't be able to deal if I lost the other. I wasn't in love with Brad. My heart always belonged to Eric, and I wasn't looking to change that any time soon, but I loved Brad like a brother. He was and is the brother I always wanted but never had.

Twenty

Eric

"I CAN'T FUCKING do this!" My fingers ball into fists and I'm about to start swinging.

This was a bad idea.

"You have to." Parker holds up his hands, palms out. As if that's going to calm me down and stop me from seeing my girl. "This is how we keep her safe from the club."

"It's also how we keep *your* ass alive," Mike adds, leaning against the brick wall.

"You agreed to this," Jay reminds me, handing me another beer.

"Fuck, I know. But I'm going crazy not being able to see her. It makes me sick that she thinks I'm dead."

"It's the safest thing for her to believe right now." Mike crosses his arms over his chest.

"Did you have to have a funeral though? That shit's kinda morbid."

Parker shrugs. "We needed them to believe you had died in that warehouse."

"Did they show at least?" I ask, after swallowing a mouthful of my beer.

"They did," Jay confirms. "So did your dad."

"Can't believe my own father fucked me over." My eyes narrow as soon as they find Parker's. "You know Alice is never going to forgive you for faking my death and funeral."

Mike chuckles from across the room. "She already hates us. Hasn't spoken a word to us since the day you were shot. Girl can hold a grudge."

Parker and Jay's lips thin. I know it's killing them that Alice has cut them out. At least she hasn't totally cut out Danielle and Katherine too.

"You should know that Brad seems to be sticking around as well," Cole adds.

I nod. "My brother's not stupid. He's going to figure out sooner or later that I'm not dead."

"Just let us do our job, and stay out of sight. The sooner we can catch these bastards, the sooner you get to come home," Mike replies.

"How much longer?" I try and fail to keep the frustration out of my voice.

Jay answers first. "Shouldn't be too much longer. With the intel Mark and Cole have gathered we're hoping to have you reunited with your girl in another month or two."

"How's the healing going?" Parker nods towards where the bullet entered my chest.

I shrug it off. "Still hurts like a bitch, but doc says it's looking good."

"Have you given any more thought to our offer?"

"What? To join your private security company?"

Heads nod all around as I meet five sets of eyes. I *had* given it a lot of thought. It was a legit job, one that didn't require me to deal in drugs, weapons, or human trafficking. According to Parker, it paid fucking great, too, and it would allow me to stay around Alice. But after she found out that my death was fake, she might not want me around after all.

I wasn't sure what I even brought to the table in terms of skill. Parker's ex special ops, mostly specializing in explosives. Jay has the best sniper score ever seen, and that's including some of the snipers in the military. He can disassemble and assemble a gun with his eyes closed. You wouldn't know Mark was there until he was already on you. Cole is great with blending in with his surroundings, he can become anyone he wanted to. And Mike was the muscle. He may not look like much, but the guy was strong. He had no problem getting anyone to talk.

And me? Nine years undercover in one of the most ruthless motorcycle clubs wasn't much to brag about. Although, I hadn't technically been undercover for more than eight years. I was fucking abandoned by my government. Shit got too real, and they bailed, but failed to get in contact with me. When I found out these guys Cole was introducing me to were law enforcement, I hesitated. I didn't trust anyone associated with any government agency anymore. But they turned out to be pretty upstanding dudes, and I'd happily die by their sides, or die protecting them.

After years of very little intel on the club to take back to the agency, I finally had the information they needed. A sense of hope filled me at the thought that this was finally over. After handing over the information I now held in my hands I would be free to go back home to Oceanview. Back to Alice.

I was a stupid teenager when I left, and should've told her how I felt before I bordered that plane. I had harbored feelings towards my best friend since her fifteenth birthday. She had planned a small get together with some of the kids from our grade but no one had showed. It had angered me that people could be so damn selfish and not show up for something when they said they would.

I did the only thing I could think of to try and rectify the situation. I cashed in what little money I had saved the previous summer and took her to dinner at one of the fancier restaurants in town. We stuffed ourselves full of Italian food and danced. And I'll never forget the sound of her laughter that night, or the way it made me want to do everything in my power to hear it again.

Steeling my nerves I type out the number I've had memorized for the better part of eight years and send the usual standard text telling him I needed to meet.

I was expecting an immediate reply with a time and place to meet the agent who has been my contact at the agency since this whole thing started, but as my phone dings with an incoming message, it's not the reply I was hoping for.

Message failed.

I check the number and try again, thinking maybe I had typed it in wrong. But I get the same response. Message Failed.

Frustrated, I hit the call button but instead of ringing, an automated voice fills my ears.

"The number you are trying to reach is unavailable. Please hang up and try your call again."

My hands start shaking as I reach inside the hidden pocket in my wallet for the piece of paper I slipped in there years ago. My eyes wander over the number scribbled across the paper to the number typed into my phone. I double check the previous received messages.

It all matches.

I try calling again, hoping that there was a mistake and the line was just busy but it doesn't ring once before the same automated voices says, "the number you are trying to reach is unavailable. Please hang up and try your call again."

Fuck my life.

This cannot be happening. Not now. The only contact number I had for my 'handler' and it wasn't in service. Of course there were any number of reasons why it wasn't working; phone got cut off, the phone died, the agent was no longer active. But deep down I knew that it was none of them.

I had read about governments just abandoning their agents in the middle of a mission but I always thought it was a media stunt, that there was no way that would actually happen. But it does. Because my government just fucking abandoned me in the middle of my one and only mission.

Without a way out, if the MC ever found out what I had been doing I was as good as dead.

Fuuck!

"If we all make it out of this alive, I'll join your team." After draining the rest of my beer, I toss the empty bottle in the recycling and grab my bike keys, shutting the memory down before it can go further. My gaze lands on and connects with Parker's, then Jay's, and I scowl. "You fuckers better keep her safe. I'm trusting you with her."

Two months, tops, then I get my girl back in my arms.

August couldn't fucking come fast enough. I was done beating around the bush and ignoring what I felt. Once I had

Alice back in my arms I was going to tell her how much I loved her, and I didn't give a fuck if that made me a pussy. Life was too short to not tell the people you love what they mean to you. And Alice, she means the fucking the world to me.

Twenty-one

Alice

"I'M HAPPY YOU called, A." Kat reaches across the counter to pick up her coffee before she turns and leads us to a table on the patio.

"Me too, Kat."

It's been a month since Eric's funeral. After everyone had left that day I recoiled into my own bubble. Except, I wasn't alone this time round.

Brad was with me.

It started out as him coming over to cook dinner for us and to make sure that I didn't spend all day in bed. One night turned into two which turned into three and before we knew it we had spent every night of the past month eating dinner together.

It was like we were each other's lifeline. Making sure neither of us retreated fully into ourselves. We leaned on each other, propped each other up, and forced each other to live every day. We may not be blood, but family didn't necessarily mean related by blood either. Family are the people who are there to pull me up and fight for me and with me when I can't pull myself up or fight for myself. They're the ones who acknowledge that I may be hurting but there is still a life to live. They're the ones who lend me their strength without being asked and without reward.

And Brad and I, we were family.

But now it was time for us to try and stand on our own, to reintegrate back into life without Eric. That's what led me to calling Kat and asking her to meet me for coffee. I still wasn't ready to face the guys, but this was a stepping stone.

"How are you doing?" Kat shifts uncomfortably in her chair. I know she's trying to be the supportive friend but has no idea where to start.

I sigh, looking down at the ice cubes floating in my iced coffee.

"It's weird, you know? I still wake up expecting to see him next to me but he's not there, and then everything comes crashing down. But for those first few seconds it's like my heart refuses to accept that he's gone."

Kat's eyes soften and an apologetic smile spreads across her face. Her lips part like she's about to say something but then gets interrupted by a high-pitched squeal. Her eyes snap to the offender, a confused look crosses her face when she looks back at me.

I turn slowly in my seat, my eyes landing on long, dark, cherry red hair and then connect with a pair of pale green eyes. I can barely contain my excitement when I jump up and almost dump my coffee on my pants.

"Alice Johnson, is that really you?" Allison asks, pushing her way through the throng of tables.

"Hi, Allie." I smile, reaching out and pulling her into a hug.

I should feel guilty that I never held up my end of the bargain and stayed in touch with the gang after I left Oceanview, but right now I was just happy to see my old friend. The guilt would come later, I was sure.

"You're a redhead." I brush my fingers through the tips of her hair, laughing.

"I was tired of the blonde." She shrugs, looking down at Kat.

"Oh sorry. Kat this is Allison. We went to high school together. Allie, this is Kat."

"Nice to meet you." Allie extends her hand towards Kat to shake.

"Join us." I insist, already pulling over a chair for her to sit down.

After we've ordered another round of coffees and donuts, Allie places a hand over mine and leans in closer to me.

"I heard about Eric. I'm so sorry, A."

I still have no idea what an appropriate response is to that so I smile and nod. We spend the better part of the next hour telling Kat stories about the three of us and our group in high school. Allison retells the story about skinny dipping in the lake and getting caught, and then Logan's reaction a few years later at the bonfire.

I learned that shortly after I left, Logan and Stacey left too. And the last Allison heard, Logan was a doctor in Seattle, and Stacey owned a little coffee shop on the Oregon Coast. It broke my heart to learn that neither of them really kept in touch either, and the little updates Allison knew were from following them on Facebook.

"So, what have you been up to, Allie?"

She grins. "The better question would be what haven't I been up to?"

Kat and I laugh. Allison was always the more free-spirited one of the group.

"I'm actually only back in town for a couple months before taking off again for a life at sea."

"Life at sea?" Kat asks.

Allie nods. "I've been working on this ship called the *Ocean Fighter.*"

Kat coughs and almost chokes on her coffee after hearing the name of the ship.

"You work on the *Ocean Fighter?*" She stares at Allie, dumbfounded.

"I do."

All I can do is giggle at where this is heading. Kat has been passionate about one of their causes, almost to the point of being kind of obsessive. And now she's found someone who works on the very same ship. I'm not sure Kat could fangirl any harder if she tried. I pick up my coffee from the table and settle into the back of my seat with a knowing smile.

"The cove is something I've been very passionate about ever since I saw the documentary. Actually, my fiancé and I ended up cutting one of their nets one year."

Allie chuckles. "I heard their nets got cut. They lost an entire pod that night."

A big smile spreads across Kat's face, and I want to tell her to not smile so hard or her face could get stuck that way, but the revving of a motorcycle catches my attention.

Across the street are several bikes, and sitting atop a couple of them are men with the Knights' MC patch on their cuts. My blood boils and my hands tighten into fists until my knuckles are turning white.

The sensible part of my brain is telling me to sit tight and let the guys handle the club. But the other part, the darker part of me wants to see them pay. Then my eyes land on a tall figure throwing a leg over his own bike.

I change my mind. I don't want to make just anyone pay. I want to make *him* pay. He stole something from me, ripped my heart in two with a pull of a trigger, and without second thought.

Prison would be too merciful of a punishment for him. No, he doesn't get to spend the rest of his life rotting behind bars. He needs to know exactly what he put Eric through. He needs to experience every stab, every burn, every gunshot. And this time he will be the one begging for death.

Clearing my throat, I gather my purse and stand. "I forgot I had told Brad I'd swing by. I'll catch up with you ladies later."

I don't wait for them to respond before pushing my way through the crowded tables and out to my car. Allison gave me her number earlier and I make a mental note to give her a call and see if she wants to do drinks later.

Then I push her and Kat, and everyone else from my mind as I throw my car into drive and follow behind the club.

Twenty-two

Alice

MY ARMS ARE from being held up my wrists, exactly like Eric had been. Except he was fully clothed, and my shirt is lying in tatters on the floor, and my pants are the only thing keeping me from being completely, and utterly naked. The rope binding my wrists together pull tighter with every movement I make.

How I ended up here is all a blur. I remember following the club to one of the chapter's clubhouses. I remember following them in, then Grim's hand gripping my neck from behind and him snarling into my ear. *And here I thought I'd have to track you down, little girl. Must be my lucky day.* Then my world went blank.

So, okay. Maybe following a MC into an unknown location by myself was not the smartest idea. But it was my need for revenge that was driving my actions, not the sensible part of my brain.

My head snaps up when I hear a chuckle from the one darkened corner of the warehouse. When I came to there was nobody here. At least I thought there had been nobody here, now I'm not so sure. How long has he been watching me struggling against my bindings? And when the fuck did they cut my shirt.

"You can try all you want, but there are only two ways you're leaving this warehouse."

As he talks he slowly emerges from the shadows. He's tall, like Eric and Brad. His hair is dark as night, like theirs too. The only difference is in the eyes. Brad's and Eric's still had a light shining in them, but this man in front of me. There's only death in his.

He stops within a few inches of me, his gaze slowly raking down my half naked body. When he reaches out a hand to graze across the top of my breasts I want to recoil in disgust, but my bindings prevent it.

"You'll either leave here as my personal whore, or you leave in a body bag. The choice is yours, little one. Choose wisely."

"Fuck you," I spit. There's no way in hell I'd ever agree to be his little plaything. I'd rather choose death a thousand times over.

Tom Knight grabs my face, digging his thumb, index, and middle fingers into my cheeks.

"I intend to." He tilts my head back, licking his way up my neck. "By the time you leave here you'll either be pleading for death or for my cock."

I whimper when his fingers pull on my nipples, and curse when they harden into peaks.

Tom grins. "So responsive. No wonder Eric could never give you up."

"You sonofabitch. You don't get to talk about Eric. His name does not get to leave your lips. I will kill you for what you did to him."

Another chuckle comes from behind me before rough hands are digging into my hips, and I feel a warm breath against my ear.

"You're not in a position to be making demands, little girl."

His hands leave their grip my hips and run up the length of my body, wrapping around my breasts.

"Damn, Prez. She's got a set of tits on her. Can I fuck her?"

"Not yet, brother. I need to check on the shipment down by the docks. When I come back we'll take turns." He smirks when the color drains from my face.

"I mean it, Grim." He stops before pushing open the door. "Don't start the fun without me," he warns, before disappearing.

"It's just you and me now, little girl." He wraps my hair around his fist and yanks my head back, burying his nose in my neck and taking an audible breath. "Prez said I couldn't fuck you, but he didn't say anything about touching."

The hand still wrapped around my breast trails down the middle of my stomach to the waistband of my pants. When I struggle against his touch, Grim yanks harder on my hair, holding me in place as he pops open the button and slides his hand under the band of my panties.

I close my eyes and will my body to not respond. This cannot be happening. I promise myself that when I get my hands free, not only will I avenge Eric's death, but I will cut off Grim's balls and feed them to him, one by one. When his fingers touch my clit, I retreat further into myself, embracing the darkness waiting below the surface.

Our family doesn't like to talk about it, but my uncle was the head of the Irish mob. Mom refused to live that lifestyle and moved away from New York straight out of high school. She met my dad shortly after starting college here in Canada. They tried to keep it from me for the longest time, but on one of our family vacations to the States, I had accidentally seen things I knew I wasn't supposed to. My uncle saw me and promised to tell me everything I wanted to know when I was older.

***

Muffled voices sound from down the hall. I have a feeling that I should run in the opposite direction and not be walking curiously toward the voices. I can't describe why I feel as if I should be running away but I know that whatever I find on the other side could possibly change my life as I know it.

I pause just outside the door that leads to the basement and debate on whether or not I should turn around. Before I can make up my mind, the door swings open with my uncle on the other side. His eyes widen in shock at seeing me standing in the hall and he hurries to close the door behind him but not before my eyes take in everything at the bottom of the stairs.

A man tied to a chair in the middle of a darkened room, beaten and bloody. Killian, my uncle's closest friend standing in front of the man with a pair of pliers. He doesn't see me when my uncle opens the door and the last image I have is of Killian leaning towards the man, gripping his finger between the metal of the pliers and the ear-piercing scream that follows right before the door clicks shut.

"Alice," my uncle says, his eyebrows drawn down in a frown.

"Uncle," I respond, trying to swallow past the dryness in my throat.

***

And he did, when the family came for a visit before I turned eighteen and left for school. But I refused to believe it. I didn't want to believe my family could be so sinister, that there was this secret that would always follow us. Even though my own family wasn't a part of it, it would still always be a big part of who we were.

I didn't want to believe it, until I needed his help. See, I had lied to Dani and Kat when I told them Mike had helped us secure an apartment when we needed to flee from Dani's ex. It wasn't Mike who helped get us set up, it was my uncle and his connections. Yes, Mike and the guys had protected us, and it was them who eventually found her when Adam took her. But she also had the Irish mob watching her back, and if the guys hadn't found Adam when they did, the mob would have.

That's where the darkness in me came from, and that's where I retreated when Grim put his hands on me. I would get my revenge, I had O'Byrne blood coursing through my veins after all.

"I have to pee," I blurt out when Grim's fingers travel further down past my clit. "If you don't want me to pee on you then I have to go pee." I silently plead with him to let me down so I can go to the bathroom and give my arms a reprieve from being hung up.

"I'm not falling for it, little girl."

"Please," I beg. "I really do need to pee."

Grim pauses, probably weighing the consequences of not letting me go and continues his assault. Finally, he withdraws his hand from my pants and eases his grip around my hair.

"If you try to run, I will kill you," he hisses in my ear before walking over to the wall and reeling me down.

Thankfully, he lets me relieve myself in peace, and as I'm making my way back to my captor, a fleck of light reflects off a piece of metal. It's sharp enough to do just the right amount of damage so I grab it and quickly stash it in my pocket and pick up one of the loose pieces of wood from a pallet and hide it behind my back.

Fight or die time, Alice.

Before I'm about to round the corner, sounds of a scuffle has me freezing in place against the wall. I'd rather not walk back out there if Tom was back and angry at Grim for letting me down. But then the sweet sounds of someone barking out a demand in Gaelic has me dropping the wood and moving out from my hiding spot. I had no idea how he found me but I didn't care.

"Ah, there you are, *neacht.*" *Niece.*

My uncle motions for one of his men to take off their suit jacket and hand it to me so I can cover up my half naked body, which I graciously accept.

When I look up again, I notice for the first time that two of his men are holding Grim up under his arms, and my uncle is in the process of rolling his sleeves up to his elbows. It would be so easy for me to let him do whatever he wanted to Grim, and sit back to watch it all happen. But some part of me knew that watching it wouldn't be the same as being the one who dealt the blows. Grim had taken so much from me, I felt it was only right that I make him pay.

"Uncle." I take a step forward and place myself between him and an unconscious Grim. "Could I...May I..." *God, why was this so hard to say? Was I really ready to take this step, to cross the line I knew there was no coming back from?*

"Spit it out, Alice," he demands.

I take a deep breath, square my shoulders, and look him straight in the eyes. "I'd like to be the one to have a chat with him."

I watch as his eyebrows raise to his hair line, and I think I've succeeded in making him speechless. But then he steps toward me and cups my face. "Are you sure, *neacht*? This is not something you should do lightly. Taking a life...it changes a person."

I let out the breath I was holding and nod. "He took away the one man I loved, Uncle. He took Eric away from me. Please, I need to be the one who does this. If someone had taken Aunt B away from you, you would want to be the person who avenged her." I plead with him to understand why I needed to be the one who does this.

"*Ta*, I wouldn't stop until their blood was on my hands."

Eyes so much like my own and my mom's search mine before he nods behind me and removes his hands from my face.

"Killian will stay. Don't worry, he will stay in the shadows," he adds when I go to protest.

My uncle places a kiss on my forehead before nodding to the two other men who finished tying Grim to a chair. They leave without another word and a backward glance. When I look around the room again, Killian is nowhere to be found. I visibly shiver with the realization that he can see and hear me and everything I do but I have no idea where he is.

I was planning on avenging Eric's death and teaching Grim a lesson. Like Tom said, there was only one way I was leaving this warehouse, and it was not in a body bag or as his whore. I was leaving victorious, and Grim was the one leaving in a body bag.

The fucker took the love of my life away from me, and he was going to pay.

A life for a life.

I was about to reenact every slice, every stab, every burn that he had ever inflicted on Eric since the time he was fifteen until Grim killed him, and then I was going to add some of my own.

The metal push cart in the corner caught my eye and I noticed that all of Grim's tools are still laid out on it. My lips thin in a slow smirk. We were going to see exactly who was the Grim Reaper now.

Payback was going to be a painful bitch.

Twenty-three

ERIC

"**B**RAVO TEAM, ARE you a go?" Parker's voice comes through my ear piece.

"Affirmative," Cole replies.

We were finally about to take down my dad and his club for human trafficking and I couldn't fucking wait. When today was over I would be free to go back to my girl.

A blacked-out van pulls up to the doors of the warehouse, Grim jumps out of the drivers' side while my dad pulls open the side door. And then my world stopped when I watched as they dragged someone out from the van and into the warehouse.

She's not conscious, and from the little viewpoint I have, it looks like her shirt is only being held onto her body by the sleeves, the front hanging open to expose her breasts to any prying eyes.

I want to propel forward and go after those sonsofbitches, but the pressure of Cole and Mark's hands on either of my shoulders forces me to stay put. When I turn my murderous glare on the man who was supposed to have my back he shakes his head, pointing to his earpiece.

"Parker wants us to hold tight. He doesn't think they'll do anything to her right now with the shipment arriving any second."

He's right. I know he's right. But when the door swings open again and my dad walks out with no Grim in sight the hairs on the back of my neck stand up, knowing from past experiences that Dad probably told Grim to hold off until after they've sorted out the shipment, but also knowing Grim doesn't listen so well to orders. When he has his mind set on something, he goes for it.

If he touches a hair on her head I swear I'll rip him limb from limb.

"The rest of the club just rolled in," Austin relays from his perch on the roof. I had only met him this morning, but Parker and Jay thought it would be a good idea to bring in some of the guys from all three teams to get as much of the docks covered as we could. We didn't want the club members sneaking under our radar.

With great difficulty, I force myself to focus on taking down this human trafficking ring and staying alert. I wouldn't be able to help Alice if I was actually dead.

Forcing myself to do something that goes beyond every bone in my body is fucking hard. Once the club members opened the doors to the shipping container we stormed them. One by one, they were each handcuffed and dragged away. The entire time we had them surrounded all I could think about was Alice and getting to her before Grim broke her.

No matter how many times I've looked in the shipping container before now, I still will never get the scene or the smell from my mind. It didn't matter how hard, or how much I scrubbed every inch of my body in the shower. It didn't matter how many times I got lost in the bottom of a bottle to make myself forget. I will always remember the horror-stricken eyes of the women and children as we opened the doors of the container further to let more light in. I will always remember the smell of human waste and death as it rose up to greet my nose.

That pain, that anger, that guilt of not being able to save them all. You never fucking forget that shit. That shit stays with you until your last breath. It feeds that drive in you to do better, to be better.

As I look around the dock at all the faces of the club members, I realize that the two men who are most responsible for all of this are nowhere to be found. Somehow, my dad and Grim have evaded capture.

A.J. Daniels

And then I hear the sound of a man's cry pierce the air.

Twenty-four

Alice

"**YOU HIT LIKE** a girl," he smirks, not caring that he's completely tied up and at my mercy.

I cock a hip and place a hand on it.

"Why, thank you." Sarcasm dripped from my voice.

Why is that men seem to think that's an insult. I'm fucking proud to be a female. Being a female didn't have to mean you're weak. You have to have some sort of strength to deal with all the hormones we have going on, on the daily.

It is not easy. Our bodies go through so much on a daily basis, and that's not including what we put ourselves through to look and feel attractive for the opposite sex.

Our bodies are made to grow a tiny human. There is no weakness in that, but yet, there are still statements like 'you hit like a girl.' *It's fucking bullshit!*

Pussies are not weak. But I'll tell you what is weak. Balls. One swift kick to those things and you can bring a grown ass man to his knees and make him cry.

I scoff. 'You hit like a girl'? Damn right I do. I mentally shake myself. I was here for a reason, and his statement and the way he's laughing make me that much more willing and excited for the lesson I was about to teach.

"You think this is amusing?" I grip the top of his man-bun in my fist and yank his head back.

"Little girl, you don't scare me," Grim snarls, his eyes darting down to my breasts. "But, we could make this interesting. Just submit to me. Let me fuck you, and I promise to make sure the other brothers don't get their hands on that tight body of yours."

I push his head back and make my way back over to the metal cart where all of his favorite torture devices are laid out for me.

That's when I spot it.

The guys said that the puncture wounds on Eric's torso were made by a pick-like device. Kind of like the push pick lying right in front of me. Grinning, I pick it up and slowly turn around. Making sure that he gets a good look at the tool I'm twirling between my fingers.

Grim clears his throat. "Those are big boy tools. Better put it down before you hurt yourself, little girl. Wouldn't want to scar up that pretty body of yours."

A smirk pulls at the corner of my mouth when I look up at him from under the wall of dark hair that had fallen in my face. Still twirling the pick between my fingers, I make my way over to where he's sitting, making sure to add a little extra sway to my hips.

Grim licks his lips and tilts his head back when I straddle him. It takes everything in me to not shiver in disgust and move away from him, but I need to teach him a lesson. I need to teach him that women are not objects, they aren't possessions, and they definitely are not toys for him to do whatever the fuck he wanted with.

I lean forward, brushing my lips against his ear, making sure to press my breasts into his chest. "Tell me more. How would you make me submit to you?" I make sure to add a raspiness to my voice.

As soon as I feel him growing hard beneath me and he tilts his hips I have to force back the bile working its way up my throat.

"First, you need to untie me."

"Awwww, but where's the fun in that? Tell me." I trail the sharp end of the pick down his torso as he tells me exactly what he would do to me if I untied his hands.

How he would push me face down on the hard floor, rip my pants off, and push my face into the cold ground as he takes me from behind.

I squeeze my eyes closed against the images he's creating and force myself to take a cleansing breath, but Grim mistakes it for me being turned on from his words and thrusts up making me feel every inch of the growing bulge behind his zipper.

I've had enough. I can't play this game anymore. I stand, still running the pick down his middle, and when I get down to the bulge in his pants, I push the head of the pick in with as much strength as I can muster, then rip it out. Grim throws his head back and screams as blood coats the front of his pants.

"You bitch!" he screams when I walk around the back of his chair. "You crazy bitch. You stabbed my dick!"

I lean down and laugh in his ear. "You ain't seen nothing yet. See, you took away someone very important to me. And this," I drag the pick up his shirt, wiping his blood off in the process. "This is payback...*bitch*." I twist the pick into his torso, and pull it out again before repeating the motion until the patches of blood match the ones on Eric's torso when I found him. In this very warehouse.

"Eric was a rat. He deserved everything I gave him and more."

"And you deserve worse for what you did to those women and children." I walked back over to the metal table replacing the push pick with metal pliers.

"They wanted it. They practically begged for it."

"They begged you to rape them?" I ask, walking back over to him, swinging the pliers in my hand.

"You're playing with fire, little girl."

"Maybe, but I'm not the one tied to a chair."

Pulling the pocket knife from my skirt, I flip open the blade and rip his shirt down the middle. Grim's eyes go wide when the cool metal of the pliers touches his nipple.

"Do you know who you're messing with, little girl? I will fucking destroy you. I will break you," he snarls.

An odd sense of calm washes over me before I respond. "Not if I destroy you first." I close the pliers around his nipple, but before I can pull it and continue my torture I hear the sound of the door to the warehouse being pulled open again.

I'm not sure what made me automatically react the way I did next, but I don't think twice about it, I just react and hurl the knife at the dark figure walking toward us. There was no way it would be anyone other than Tom Knight. My uncle is not so stupid to walk back into the warehouse without at least having Killian warn me.

A high-pitched cry leaves the tall figure before it doubles over and crumbles to the ground. I take a few hesitant steps toward it, and smirk to myself when Tom Knight comes into my view. The blade of my pocket knife lodged squarely into, what I can only assume, are his balls. I can't help but be impressed. I was not aiming for that area when I threw the knife. Hell, I wasn't even aiming at all. Looks like my bad aim worked in my favor for once.

I turn to make my way back to Grim when the doors are pried all the way open again, followed by a sound I thought I would never hear again.

Get it together, Alice. You can't be losing your shit now.

I'm pretty sure I'm going crazy but I shake it off and start twisting the pliers again. I hear that same familiar sound repeat amongst Grim's curses. I had figured Killian was the reason the door had opened again, but I was sorely mistaken.

When I turn around to find the source of the voice, the pliers fall from my fingers, and I feel like someone punched me in the gut. Because staring back at me, surrounded by at least ten other men dressed in tactical gear, are the very eyes I've come to know as well as my own.

But it can't be him, because I buried him. I watched as they lowered his body into the ground. I watched the life leave his eyes.

Jay and Mark push forward from behind him. Jay picks up the pliers from the floor while Mark walks over to Grim and starts checking him over. While Cole and Mike walk over to where Tom is still lying.

I vaguely hear Mark and Jay curse as they take stock of each of Grim's injuries. My lips quirk in a small smirk for a split second before the realization of who is currently standing in front of me crashes down on me. My brain still refuses to acknowledge what my heart already knows.

"Eric?"

"Hi, babe."

"Y-You're dead."

I don't know what else to say so I stand there, like an idiot, staring at him with my mouth gaping open. There is so much I want to ask, like how is he here right now? Why is he not dead? But most importantly... *What the actual fuck is going on?*

And like he always has, he reads my mind when he reaches out, running his knuckles down the side of my face and whispers, "I'll answer all your questions later."

"Well, well. The rat isn't dead after all. Better scurry along before the rest of the brothers find out you're alive," Grim warns while being led away in cuffs.

"You mean the ones with their faces in the dirt being handcuffed outside?" Another familiar voice says behind Eric.

We both turn towards the new voice at the same time, and Eric looks as shocked as I feel when Brad walks further into the room and out of the shadows.

"Someone please tell me what the fuck is going on?" I bark, but when no one makes a move to explain anything to me I barely refrain from throwing a kid's size temper tantrum and instead make a beeline for the door.

Twenty-five

ERIC

"**B**RAD? WHAT THE fuck?"
He grins, holstering his weapon and throws an arm around my shoulder. "Hey, little brother."

"You're military?"

How the fuck did I not know that my brother was in the military?

"We'll talk later. And you'll tell me just how, exactly, you also came to be undercover, and for CSIS no less. For now, go get your girl, and don't let her get away."

I nod. He was right, we had a lot to discuss. Like how neither of us knew the other was working for the government, except I wasn't anymore. Hadn't been for years. But that shit could wait. I needed to go comfort my girl. Alice had never tortured someone before, and while she was still running on the adrenaline rush, she is bound to crash, and I'm guessing it would be soon.

I was proud as fuck of my girl though, and I was right. She did go toe-to-toe with the president of the Knight's MC, and she fucking won. She did more than win, she made him cry like a fucking bitch.

I was a sick, sadistic, sonofabitch if I got turned on knowing my girl had tortured Grim. But to be fair, she had warned them she was out for blood and would avenge my death. And I don't completely blame them for not believing her, Alice didn't grow up in this violent lifestyle. She has two loving parents and an upstanding childhood. But I had a feeling there was more to that story than even she was letting on. What they failed to realize, was that they took away the one person she loved more in this life than her parents.

Me.

And Alice was fiercely protective over those she loved. She may not have grown up in this violent lifestyle, but that didn't mean that she wouldn't embrace it to protect. People did things out of character for themselves when someone they loved was hurt. Alice was not only avenging my death, but every bit of torture I experienced at the hands of those two men. And I loved her even more for it.

I prayed she wouldn't lose herself to it, though. After getting that first taste of blood, it becomes addictive. Whenever someone wrongs me my first thought will always be revenge. It was a dark way to live, and I didn't want that darkness to take over who she was. She was my light, and I vowed to do everything I could to make sure she never had to take a person's life as long as I lived.

"You okay?" I ask as I walk up to where she's sitting in the ambulance, but keep my distance.

I wasn't sure how she was going to react to me not being dead. It had only been less than an hour since she found out, and I didn't want to push her right now.

"I'm fine." Her tone is clipped and to the point, and she doesn't try making eye contact with me, instead choosing to watch the paramedic bandage her wrists.

"You're good to go. Just keep the bandages on until the burns start to heal," the paramedic concludes, taking off her gloves and moving on to the next person.

"Alice," I start.

"Don't." She stands and starts walking away, only to stop a few feet ahead. "Take me home, please." She throws the words over her shoulder, still refusing to look at me, and makes her way back to my truck.

I'm in so much shit.

Twenty-six

ERIC

WE DON'T MAKE it more than two feet past her front door before her hand comes up and her palm connects with the side of my face almost making me see stars.

Fuck, I forgot how strong she was.

In the next second after her hand leaves my face, both of her hands tangle in the front of my shirt pulling me closer to her. Her lips meet mine in a searing kiss, and I groan when she pushes her soft body against mine.

"This doesn't mean that I forgive you," her mouth says one thing, but her body is saying something completely different.

We're a tangle of limbs as we pull at each other's clothes making our way to her bedroom.

"You should've told me." Her back arches off the bed as I trail kisses down her stomach.

"Was trying to protect you, babe."

Her breath hitches when my tongue finds her clit. Her fingers tangle in what little hair I have left and holds me to her.

"I can protect myself, Eric."

My lips leave her clit to trail wet kisses back up to her breasts where my tongue circles each nipple before finding her mouth again. Whatever response I had to her comment gets swallowed by her when she refuses to end the kiss.

Without breaking contact, I slide into her inch by inch earning a low moan from her. I could get used to spending every day like this, right here with the woman who has always held my heart.

And for the rest of the night, I prove to her exactly how much I love her.

***

As morning light streams through the cracks of the blinds in her room I take that opportunity to look down at the woman who owns me. Heart, body, and fucking soul.

I didn't sleep at all the night before. Preferring to savour the feel of her in my arms, her head on my shoulder, her breath on my skin. There were moments, after being shot, in the ambulance, and while in surgery, where I thought I was a goner. I should've been. I had lost too much blood, I should've died in that warehouse, and again on that surgery table. But all I could think about was never seeing Alice again. Never hearing her laugh, never hearing her bitch me out, never feeling her heat surround me. And I refused to die without telling her I loved her, that I had been in love with her my whole fucking life.

Walking back into the room after a shower, my cock stiffens at the sight that greets me. Alice is still asleep on her stomach, the sheet barely concealing her beautiful body from my view.

She was the one I had held out for. While being the son of the president of an MC got me as many women as I wanted, there was only one I craved.

While she allowed me to dominate her in the bedroom, I would never force myself on a woman like my father and the rest of the members did, but my time with them meant nothing. Fucking them was a means to temporarily cure the craving. Alice was the one I wanted, the one I craved. She would always be the one I craved.

Dropping my towel, I crawl back up the bed, kissing my way from the small of her back, moving her hair away from the nape of her neck and licking up the slight curve. My teeth gently tug at her ear lobe, earning me a moan from those soft pouty lips.

"Eric," she moans, sleep clouding her voice when I dip a finger into her pussy, her hips lifting slightly to allow me more access.

She starts riding my hand wildly when I add a second, then third finger, meeting each of my thrusts with her own. Her moans and screams permeate the air when I press my thumb to her clit. And nip and suck along her neck and shoulder, adding to the onslaught. Her pussy constricts around my fingers and I know she's close.

"Come for me, baby. Show me how much you want my cock. Coat my fingers in your come," I whisper in her ear.

Alice throws her head back against my shoulder and screams my name as she does what she's told and comes hard while I finger fuck her.

I don't wait for her to come down from her orgasm before I'm slamming into her from behind. Lifting her hips until she's on all fours, wrapping her long hair around my fist tugging her head back.

"Come for me again, Alice. Scream my name, baby."

And she does, over and over again while I slam into her almost violently, losing myself in her.

I collapse back on the bed next to her, my breaths coming in heavy pants when she lifts my arm and curls into my side. I could get used to mornings like this.

"Don't think because you can fuck me like that, that I'll forget we need to talk," she says, tracing my tattoos and the new scars that adorn my torso.

I chuckle, running the tips of my fingers up and down her arm. "Yes ma'am."

"I watched you die in my arms." Her voice cracks at the memory. "I watched you being lowered into that grave."

Fuck, I'm an asshole.

"I know."

She pulls out from under my arm and grabs the sheet around her body, moving to sit on the edge of the bed with her back to me. "Was that part of the plan all along?"

"It was never part of the plan." Moving behind her, I sweep her hair off her shoulder and trail kisses up her neck, grinning when she shivers.

Pulling away from my touch she moves quickly away from the bed. "Damnit, Eric. You can't distract me from this conversation with sex."

"Alice."

"No. Fuck you! I fucking watched you die. You died in my arms, Eric! And then I had to plan your fucking funeral, and watch you being lowered into the ground. Only to find out that you're not dead, and all you want to do is get your dick wet. My heart literally broke when you died. It fucking hurt. It hurt so much. It hurt because I realized I never fucking told you I loved you, and thought I would never be able to."

I watch as the second strongest person I know breaks in front of me. She crumbles to the floor and wraps her arms around herself as sobs shake her body. And I was the cause of it. Yeah, I was a fucking asshole for doing what I did to her.

I tip her chin back with a finger, forcing her to look at me while tears still stream down her face.

"Say it again." My voice is rough and demanding, but I need to hear her say it again.

She tries to move and look away but I grip her chin and force her to look at me again.

"Say it again, Alice."

She glares at me. "I love you, you fucking asshole. There? Is that what you want to hear?"

"Fucking right it is," I growl pressing my lips to hers and wrapping my arms around her. "I'm so fucking sorry, baby."

She buries her face in my neck and digs her nails into my back holding me in place. "Don't you dare leave me again, Eric. I buried you once, I am not burying you a second time."

"Yes ma'am." I lean back, framing her face in my hands and just look at her. She has yesterday's mascara running down her cheeks, and her hair messed up from last night's and this morning's activities, but she's still the most beautiful fucking woman on earth.

"I love you." I kiss the spot right under her ear, and each side of her mouth. "I should've told you that months, hell, even years ago."

"You're forgiven." She grins.

"Answer me one thing."

127

"Anything."

"I've never known you to get violent like that, or at all. Why--"

Alice sighs before I can finish asking my question. "My uncle is the head of the Irish Mob. I may have accidentally walked in on him while he was in the middle of torturing someone. I had just turned eighteen and he was up here visiting. I guess it was a combined personal and business trip. I learned a lot that day."

"Fuck. You have ties to the Irish mob?"

"I do. So you better not fuck up again," she teases.

"Yeah, no. I don't have a death wish." I grit my teeth. *Fuck. The Irish mob? That's some serious shit.* You don't fuck with the Knight's MC, but you definitely do not fuck with the Irish Mob, unless you have a serious death wish. And I happened to like my life the way it was...you know, *alive.*

"You don't have to worry about them, Eric."

"You realize that government agent and mob boss don't see eye to eye, right? I'm pretty sure your uncle will shoot me on the spot if we ever meet."

"He won't. Well, he promised not to."

"What?"

"I'm kidding."

"Jesus, Alice. You can't fucking joke about shit like that. He might actually kill me."

"Eric." She presses her palm to my chest and leans her forehead against mine. "You have nothing to worry about when it comes to him."

I huff, wrapping my arms more securely around her. I wasn't planning on letting go any time soon.

"What do you mean 'government agent'?"

Shit. "Caught that, did you?"

"Eric." She sighs. "I don't know if I can do any more secrets. So please, just tell me what the hell is going on."

I kiss her forehead then her lips. "Let's go make coffee, then I'll tell you everything you want to know. I need to have a talk with my brother as well."

She nods. "Seems like there are plenty of secrets to go around in your family."

I nod. "We all have a lot to talk about."

Twenty-seven

ERIC

"**HEY, LITTLE BROTHER**." Brad grins, pushing past me and walking down the hall to Alice's kitchen.

I hadn't decided yet if I wanted to buy a house or not, and since my lease on the rental apartment was up next week I was hoping Alice and I would be talking about looking for a house together, because I was not about to move into her tiny one bedroom. I was tired of living in limbo, and was ready to move our relationship to the next step.

"There she is. Hi baby girl," Brad greets Alice, walking up to her, picking her up and spinning her in a circle as she laughs. A growl leaves my chest with the way he's touching her.

"Down, boy." He laughs, placing her back on her feet. "I know she's all yours."

Alice gives me a stern look before turning to him. "Now that you're here, the two of you can man the grill." Then she saunters back into the house to grab the meat out of the fridge.

"Thanks for looking out for my girl." I tip my bottle to him and throw back the rest of my beer.

Brad shrugs. "Anytime. She's like a sister to me. I wasn't about to stand back and watch her retreat into herself after your death."

I wince at the reminder of how much Alice had been hurting after my death. I knew I would never be able to go back and undo the hurt I caused her. The only thing I could do was try and make it up to her by doing everything I can to make her happy.

"You're not pissed?" I eye my brother.

"Nah, I get it. You were trying to protect her. Can't say I wouldn't have done the same."

"So," Alice starts, handing us each another beer and making herself comfortable on my lap. "The rest of the group will be here shortly. If we're going to talk, we should do it now." She looks from me to my brother and back again. "One of you please start talking."

"My team got the call that the Oceanview ERT teams were needing more backup on a human trafficking case. We responded to the call and were there to help out." Brad doesn't elaborate anymore on his part.

"So you already knew the guys? And why did we not know that you were RCMP?" Alice asks.

She's got a fucking good point.

"Because I'm not RCMP."

"That's pretty fucking vague, Brad. What the hell do you mean you're not RCMP?"

He shrugs but doesn't respond. I've had enough. We were supposed to be family but there was nothing but secrets between us.

"Answer the damn question, brother."

He slams back the rest of his beer and reaches over for a new one before looking back over at us. "I can't. Our agency technically doesn't exist, so there's nothing to answer." He looks pointedly at me. "How about you tell us how you came to be working for CSIS."

Alice looks over at him and crosses her arms. "This conversation isn't over, Bradley." Then she turns those honey eyes on me and waits.

"They recruited me right out of high school. Said they had been following the club's activities for years but couldn't find a way in. They trained me and sent me back in. But what they failed to realize was that Dad didn't trust me with club business at first. It took years for me to earn his trust and work my way to a position at the table. Then and only then was I privy to all the information regarding the trafficking. When I finally had enough information to take back to the agency I had found out that my agent status was 'KIA.' Killed In Action. They didn't get the information they wanted during their time line so they fucking abandoned me."

"Shit." Brad sighs, leaning further into his seat.

"I'm not sure when they pulled the plug on me, but a year after I found out, I ran into Cole again. He mentioned he was part of an elite RCMP team. I was just sitting on all this information and I needed out. I didn't think I would be able to handle opening one more shipping container knowing there was nothing I could do for all those women and children.

And I wanted to get back to you, Alice. I knew I had hurt you for all those years. I needed to be free from the club before I could find you again. So Cole set up the meeting with Jay and Parker." I lean back in my chair, wrapping an arm around Alice's shoulder and pulling her back with me. "The rest is history."

"Why'd you fake your death?" Alice directs the question at me, little bits of hurt still evident in her voice.

"That wasn't part of the plan, but when Grim found us at the restaurant he said my dad had known all along that I had been scheming up ways to bring down the club. As soon as I came to after surgery, I told Parker and Jay and we decided that the best thing was for my dad and Grim to believe I was dead. We thought it would keep you safe and out of the club's radar if I was no longer around. But I should've known that as soon as Grim laid eyes on you, you were already a target for him."

Alice visibly shivers leaning further back into me. "He doesn't deserve to rot in prison for the rest of his life."

"He won't be for long," Brad mumbles under his breath before there are sounds of chaos coming from the front door and Bella is running through the back door.

"Aunt Alice, look!" She bounds up to us holding a trophy in front of her.

"What's this?" Alice leans forward so Bella can show her what the engraving says. "You made VIP?"

Bella nods, her high ponytail swinging from side to side, a wide grin on her face. "I did."

"That's so cool, Bell! So proud of you," Alice gushes, pure love and adoration for her niece in her voice.

"Didn't know they gave out trophies in her league," I ask Parker when the rest of the team joins us on the patio and Alice leads Bell back in the house to see what the girls are up to.

"Didn't know that either until Bell came home with one." Parker shakes his head. "She's hasn't let that thing out of her sight all day." There's a small smile on his face, despite his words, and I know that he couldn't have been prouder of Bella.

"So, what's the story?" Brad asks when Cole hands us each another beer from the cooler.

I have no idea what happened after I left the warehouse and brought Alice home. That was part of the reason why everyone decided to meet up today. That, and Parker was expecting my answer today on whether or not I'd be joining the security firm.

In truth, I still wasn't a hundred percent sure if I still wanted a career in law enforcement. I knew the benefits of it, and I knew that this time around would be different. These guys would never abandon me in the middle of a mission. But that didn't mean that I still didn't have my doubts.

Even though my dad and his club were successfully taken down, it didn't mean we were out of the dark. We had taken down one chapter, albeit it was the mother chapter, and for right now there was no way for us to know if another one of the chapters was going to take over, or if they had taken over already. And that is the only reason why I found myself agreeing to join the team.

Jay runs a hand through his hair. "We're still waiting to hear from the Inspector but I'm guessing your dad, Grim, and a few of the other members will be going away for a long time, especially with their records."

Twenty-eight

Alice

"**D**O YOU LOVE me?" Eric whispers into my hair.

"Always." I smile, lazily drawing circles with a finger on his exposed chest.

"How much do you love me?"

I draw in a long, slow breath looking up at him. His hair hanging haphazardly down his forehead in a way that only Eric could make look sexy as sin, a lazy smile on his face, and the love I see clear as day in his eyes makes me think that life couldn't get any better than this.

"To infinity and beyond." I grin.

It was true. Although, the actual saying was 'to the moon and back' but that seemed so limited. I could see the moon every night, and even though I knew it was a long way away, it still didn't fully encompass how much I loved this man.

But infinity, I couldn't see into infinity. It was endless. Much like my love for Eric. My love for him knew no bounds. I would walk 'til the ends of the earth for him, and then some. I would kill for him, and almost had.

Would I die for him? I don't know. I would if me dying meant that he got to live. But I'd much rather live for him. Dying was easy, but living…living was hard. I should know, I had to experience life without him in it for a second time. And it was the hardest thing I've ever had to do. I prayed that I wouldn't have to experience that kind of pain again, even while knowing that some day I would.

"Do you know how much I love you?" he asks.

"How much?"

"To infinity and beyond and back again." He grins, and I giggle when he starts tickling me.

"You don't play fair." I playfully smack his chest when he flips me over onto my back and looms over me, placing both his elbows on either side of my head.

"Oh, I play plenty fair." He lowers himself down slowly, making sure I feel every inch of his hard body.

"Not fair," I moan when his hard cock slides over my panties.

"It's you and me, babe," he says, between peppering kisses along my jaw and down my neck.

"Always and forever." I breathe, as I feel his fingers brush my panties aside before sliding into me. One delicious inch at a time.

Epilogue

ERIC

"ERIC." **MR. JOHNSON'S** voices booms next to me and I have to force myself not to squirm in my seat like I did when I was growing up.

Neil was like a father to me and Brad for the thirteen years I knew his daughter before I was forced to move. He stepped in at a time we both needed a father figure and he did everything our own dad wasn't around to do. He took us fishing on the weekends, he came to our games, he even coached my little league basketball team.

I never told Alice this but she wasn't the first person I said goodbye to so many years ago. It was Neil. I felt like I owed him that much after everything he had done for my brother and I over the years. I wasn't expecting him to tell me he was proud of me, and that he wished there was more he could've done to keep me here.

When he said that, at that moment, I decided I hated my mother with every fiber of my being. If she wasn't a junkie, I could've stayed and been a part of Alice's family. I would've still had a family, and Alice would be wearing my ring right now.

Regardless of all that though, the Johnsons welcomed me back with open arms and it felt like I had never left.

"Neil." I nod when he takes up the seat next to me. Our eyes automatically go over to where Alice is sitting talking with her mother and Dani and Kat.

"It's good to have you back, son," he says, clapping a hand on my shoulder never taking his eyes off his wife and daughter.

"It's good to be back, sir."

Seconds tick by while we watch the two most important women in our lives throw their heads back and laugh. Alice is fucking perfection when her smile reaches her eyes. It's like they light up from within.

"You're good for her," her dad comments, looking down at the beer between his fingers.

I shake my head. "It's the other way around, she's good for me. She makes me want to be a better man."

He chuckles leaning back in his chair. "Ain't that the truth. She's a lot like her mother that way."

I nod. Alice's mother was everything my own mother wasn't. She was attentive, caring, loving, stern. In short, she gave a damn about us. My mother dearest could've cared less about Brad and I.

"You love her?"

"Yes, sir, with everything I am."

He nods, looking over at his wife again, then he reaches into his pockets and pull out a black velvet box, stopping within inches of placing it in my waiting hand.

"Alice deserves the world. I saw firsthand the way she was when she thought you were dead, and I've seen firsthand the way she was when three years went by and you never came home."

I cringe at his words but he keeps talking.

"But I've also seen the way she is when she's around you. She can't help but smile. The two of you were always attached at the hip, from the time you met at three years old until you left at fifteen, then again when you came back a couple months ago. Her mom always said it'd be you she married one day, but I never wanted to believe her because that meant my baby girl was going to grow up."

His hard, dark eyes flick up to mine and I have to again force myself not to squirm under his gaze.

"But Eric, it would be an honor to have you as my son-in-law. Hell, we already consider you part of this family," he says, handing me the box.

When I flip it open and see the ring staring back at me, I feel like I've been struck dumb. I know the words I should say, the words I want to say, but none of it is coming out.

The ring is a simple yellow gold band with a cluster of diamonds sitting atop it. It's the ring I remember her mother always wearing while we were growing up. The ring Alice always said that she wanted when she got engaged. And her dad had handed it to me without me asking.

I had planned on asking him for the ring, and for his blessing in another year when I was planning on proposing, but heck, now seemed like as good a time as any.

"Sir," I clear my throat and try to come up with the words that would prove to him how I feel about his daughter.

Neil chuckles, taking a sip of his beer, and placing a hand on my shoulder. "Son, if you're about to ask for my blessing to marry my daughter there's no need. You've always had my blessing. There's no one else I would trust her heart to than you."

I nod, still trying to wrap my head around what exactly just happened here. I swallow hard and just as my eyes search out Alice she glances up at me from under long dark hair and smiles a smile that has my heart racing and my palms going sweaty.

I was finally going to do it. After all the talk of her being mine, I was finally going to make it official.

***

ALICE

F. Scott Fitzgerald once said, "Two souls are sometimes created together and in love before they're born."

I wholeheartedly believe he was talking about Eric and me. Even though we met when we were three and grew up to be really close friends until those feelings started changing when we were fifteen, I think some part of me always knew I was in love with Eric.

No other man, no other person, no other soul had ever been able to unearth the same level of feelings I felt every time Eric entered the room or I heard his voice, or someone mentioned his name. My breath hitched, my heart rate sped up, and my palms got sweaty.

It had always been him when I was fifteen.

It is always him now fourteen years later at twenty-nine.

And it will always be him until my last breath.

I waited fourteen years for him to walk back into my life, and we were going to spend the next fifty, sixty years making up for every minute lost.

Always his.

Acknowledgements

First and foremost, I'd like to thank my husband for not giving up on me and proving to me that there are still good men out there, and for being patient while I learned how to trust again.

To my brother, M, and my mom, words cannot describe how grateful I am for your encouragement and your support. I love you. M, thank you for putting up with my crazy random story ideas in the middle of the night. I'm surprised you haven't turned your phone off yet haha.

To my dad, Neil. There is not a day goes by where I don't miss you, but I know I'll see you again one day. RIP daddy. I love you.

JM Walker at Just Write. Creations, thank you so much for this beautiful cover.

Ansley Blackstock, I had a blast working with you on this story. I loved your comments throughout the editing process, especially the ones on Eric and a particular scene #sorrynotsorry.

My beta and arc readers, you ladies are amazing and I'm thankful for each and every one of you.

To the readers, you didn't have to take a chance on a new author but I'm thankful that you did. I hope you enjoyed Eric and Alice's story.

Note From The Author

I had so much fun writing Eric and Alice's story. I found myself wishing that I had more of Alice's confidence. She isn't afraid to stand up for the people she loves and she goes into every situation with her head held high.

The author has taken creative liberties with all names, places, and organizations mentioned in this book, and are not a reflection of any person, living or dead, or organization.

Always You is the third and last book in the Behind These Eyes series but each book in the series can be read as a standalone, although, it's recommended to read them in order. The Behind These Eyes series is the prequel to The Guardians series.

Playlist

"Outlaw in Me" by Brantley Gilbert
"The Fighter" by Keith Urban ft. Carrie Underwood
"More than a feeling" by Boston
"Everlasting Friend" by Blue October
"Broken" by Seether
"She's Like the Wind" by Patrick Swayze
"When You Say Nothing At All" by Ronan Keating
"All On Me" by Devin Dawson
"Issues" by Julia Michaels
"So Far Away" by Staind
"Written In The Scars" by The Script

About the Author

You can take the girl out of the ocean but you cannot take the ocean out of the girl. A.J believes that describes her to a T. She practically grew up on a beach in Cape Town, South Africa until her family immigrated to Canada. However, the ocean still has a way of relaxing her. If she can't get to the water, then a long drive with the music blaring will work just fine.

She wears her heart on her sleeve and is a self-proclaimed hopeless romantic who believes that everyone deserves their happily ever after. A.J. lives in BC, Canada with her husband. When she's not writing, she's reading. She loves the NFL and drinks way too much coffee.

If you enjoyed reading Always You, please leave a review on your favorite book retailer and/or Goodreads.

Other books by the author

Behind These Eyes series:
Skin Deep (January 2017)
Piece of Me (July 2017)
Always You (September 2017)

The Guardians series:
Brad (2018)

Standalones:
Body of Roses (2018)
Un•Breakable (2018)

CONTACT A.J:
EMAIL: **a.daniels.author@gmail.com**
FACEBOOK: **A.J. Daniels Author**
INSTAGRAM: **A.J_Daniels_Author**

www.ingramcontent.com/pod-product-compliance
Lightning Source LLC
Chambersburg PA
CBHW030307130626
46549CB00002B/741